REBELLION

JOSEPHINE BOYCE

Mary,
Welcome to The
Rebellion! .

Joseph

For Jules.
Thank you for fighting for me,
with me, and against me.

The war is over and every nation is lost. We are a region ruled by one power.

WEEK ONE

I wake up for the third time in four days with bile in my throat, the crack of gunfire once again my morning alarm. I lie still and pull the chain to switch on my light; I shut my eyes and enjoy the blindness, the oblivion, which the whiteness brings.

Outside our front door, a soldier stands surveying our street. I keep my head down and go on my way; I don't need any trouble from the Crones. As I quicken my pace, my eyes drift along the pavement where a spray of fresh blood is being cleaned up. My nails dig into my palms. My morning alarm had been an execution a few hundred metres from my home.

At the end of the road I can see a new camera being fitted. I make my way down side streets that have yet to have cameras installed.

Soon, the entire town will feel like a prison, but not yet, I tell myself, not yet.

Mum is asleep when I arrive at the hospital. She looks so small in her bed, the sheets twisted around her from a feverish night. I pause in the doorway to the ward, caught unawares by my terror; she looks so fragile, so near to... Her breathing sounds hollow as I approach and her skin is pallid. I stroke her cheek gently to wake her because I know she would hate to have missed my visit. A small smile settles on her lips when her eyes open.

Betty Clarence is kicking up some sort of a fuss, yet again. Betty has cancer, just like Mum, but Betty likes the drama that comes with such a terrible diagnosis. Betty has only one more round of chemo to go but my mum's cancer is different; it doesn't respond that well to chemo.

"How's Jake?" Mum hasn't stopped being my mum, even when the drugs made her sick, or when she was worried about my dad. She still makes sure I am okay — checks that I am eating enough and behaving well.

"He's okay... getting by as best he can." I pick at a loose thread on her blanket.

"That's not what I meant," she said, raising her eyebrows expectantly.

"Mum, stop! I told you, I don't like him like that." I pull harder at the thread.

"Yeah, yeah," she mimics.

"Besides, he's going through a really bad time and he doesn't think of *me* like that."

"Cassia, you always put yourself down." She touches my cheek affectionately. "You're beautiful in every way."

I wrinkle my nose in defiance.

"No Mum, you're beautiful. I look like Dad." I roll my eyes at her and point to my dimpled chin.

She really is beautiful, even whilst ravaged by cancer. She is petite with dark hair and a Mediterranean complexion, a long straight nose that on her looks regal, with big almond eyes and a slim face. Both my parents are Italian and so yeah, I look Italian too.

Time is up too quickly. It always goes too quickly but as I am leaving, I see Dr McMawny. He was the one who told my mum the worst news, and he'd been at her side ever since. I'd grown quite fond of him and would sometimes stay late on a Sunday to sort through his paperwork for him. He gives me a forlorn smile when he sees me approaching and runs his hand through his short, rapidly greying hair.

"Any news?" I am fidgety, anxious to know there would be a solution to my mother's illness.

"They're still not allowing us to spend our budget on buying the more expensive medicines we need, I'm sorry Cassia." He looks tired, ten years older than he did a few months ago, and, most worryingly, he looks defeated.

"Where do you buy it from?" I keep my voice level, casual.

"They have supplies in Sesellend." He begins to glance away, a signal that he has to get back to work.

"But that's just across the border!" I clench my fists in frustration; how could something so close be so hard to get?

"I know… Look, if there was anything more I could be doing, I would be doing it… short of robbing the joint." He lets out an exhausted laugh and I just manage to contain one of excitement.

"What other medicines do you need?" My desperation is too obvious, too painful for Dr McMawny to acknowledge fully.

He lets out a weary breath and looks at me tiredly. "Want a list?"

"Actually, I do — I know someone who might be able to help."

Dr McMawny takes me to his office and prints off a list that covers two sides of A4.

"Piece of cake," I say, he raises his eyebrow at me.

"I'm not going to hold my breath on this Cassia."

I give him my finest and most innocent smile and leave the hospital, a plan already forming.

Here's what I'm thinking — the town of Sesellend is about 150 miles west of the city. The Global Defence Organisation takes work details to the western border once a week to work on the farmland that remains. A lot of my old school friends have spent time there; it is hard for teenagers to adjust to new regimes. All I'd have to do is to get picked. Best way to get picked? To get into trouble.

I'd never been much of a risk taker before, but something changed the day the GDO invaded. The injustice of everything we knew being abolished, the merciless murders, the loss of those I knew and loved; that does something to you. My insides churned with frustration on a daily basis and I began to do little things to convince myself they weren't winning. Swiping a ration card from a soldier, skipping off work early with Jake, moving stuff around inside soldier camps to confuse them, sneaking out at night and pouring plaster into the toilets of the local barracks — pranks mostly, but it was leading to something. It was like I was testing myself to see how far I was willing to go.

I grew up in a city called Amphora, in a small white townhouse down Leopold Avenue. Amphora is the capital of Auria; it's an old city with a large cathedral in the centre. We lived nearer the suburbs of the city where the roads became wider, the houses larger. The city itself isn't full of glass high-rises; it's kept its charm — yellow and white houses with cool grey roofs hug one another. Ancient walls still stand in places, despite the destruction that inevitably came with the GDO occupation. Yes, other cities, like the manufacturing city of Ollen, shimmer from reflected windows that reach into the clouds, but they aren't as beautiful as Amphora.

There was a small park near my house where we'd spend most of our time during the summer months, which was down a nearby alley. I flew my first kite there, broke my first bone there, and celebrated most of my birthdays there. Now, it's a patch of mud that a few soldiers patrol after the 9pm curfew. My childhood has become a field of dirt because of them. My home is no longer my own. My teddies are used as pillows for soldiers' heads; they have desecrated everything I loved. I am seventeen but my childhood evaporated once the war broke down my country's doors.

They took my dad ten days after they invaded. They came at breakfast — we were sitting at the table like any normal family, and they led him away. Just like that. My dad worked for the government; he wasn't high up or anything, but every government official was imprisoned. I guess they thought it was safer for them that way — eliminate the established order so we have to turn to a new power for guidance. That's how it must have happened all over.

Right now, I'm living with my dad's friend Moses Kemei, his wife Mena, and their two sons, Luca and Ellyas. The flat we live in was once the ground floor of a townhouse; now it houses all five of us. There is a main living area with one sofa salvaged from the Kemeis' previous flat. The floor is wooden and creaks to alert Mena and Moses if you try to sneak out after curfew. The kitchen is simple and small but has everything Mena needs to create the best food I have ever tasted. Mena and Moses have their own room; it was once the study. They have a mattress on the floor with one of Mena's silk scarves hanging from the wall as a headboard. A small window lets in light, and whenever I'm in there I wonder how Mena can make something so small and simple feel like home.

What was once the dining room is Luca and Ellyas' bedroom. They have a single mattress each at opposite ends, and nothing hangs from their walls; I think this is partly because they refuse to accept they'll be there long. My room was once the cupboard under the stairs, but it's roomy enough for a mattress and a stack of books as a bedside table. Moses drilled holes into the door because he was worried I would suffocate in there. They didn't want me to have to sleep in such a confined space, but I insisted because I like it; it's a cocoon where I feel safe. My walls are covered with pictures of my parents, my friends, of my life before.

We only have a toilet in our flat and so we use the shower in the flat upstairs and they use our kitchen. Everyone shares everything now; in a way, I like it. I never knew so many people in the way I do now — it's like an extended family, especially because we stick together, against our common enemy.

The Kemeis are really nice people — they share out their rations with me, they've given me my own space to sleep — but it's not my family. I want my family back.

Luca, Jake, and I get up at 6am to go to work. Everyone has to contribute to the workforce now. We work as street cleaners; not exactly the most glamorous job, but at least we aren't stuck inside in a factory. There are times when there is blood to clean up, from fighting, or an execution. I try not to think about who died, or how they died.

We do our best to distract ourselves from the horror of it, but sometimes I find myself waking up believing my hands are soaked in fresh blood, that I was the murderer. But we don't talk about it. We never talk about it. We just keep going, because we have to.

Emma, Jake's twelve-year-old sister, works in a nursery looking after orphaned children, even though she's only a child herself. I'm glad she's there though, as it's something positive for her to focus on after losing her parents. I can't imagine how hard everything is for her, but at least she still has Jake.

We collect our gear from the store down old Abigail Street, now Street 41, H Sector. We wriggle into our jumpsuits and begin our day's work. We have to clean all of H Sector every day. We're supposed to split up but it's really dull doing it that way so we work as a team instead. It makes the day go quicker. Jake and I do most of the talking — we've been friends since we were six — but Luca is more of your strong silent type. He's a year older than we are but is built like a man, with warm dark skin and deep brown eyes. If I didn't know him I'd probably be afraid of him; there's something in his stature that commands respect. Jake is fairer; he has messy, short brown hair, grey eyes, and a leaner build. Ever since he lost his parents there's sadness in everything he does; he doesn't laugh any more. So, I try to help him get through every day, make it easier by distracting him and then, one day, the sadness won't be as strong and he'll start to heal.

Down a street whose name I can't remember but is now Street 54, we stop for lunch. We're not supposed to stop for lunch but there isn't a camera there, so it's our go-to lunch destination. Jake, with a flourish, lays out a cleaning rag at my feet for me to sit on.

"Why, thank you, sir," I said, putting on a fake Southern American accent.

"My pleasure, ma'am. Now, can I serve you the Spam, the Spam or the *Spam* sandwich?"

"Oh, such choice!" I fan myself with my hand and then lightly press it to his arm. "I'll take the *Spam.*"

"Excellent choice ma'am."

Luca sits down next to me, smiling.

"And for the gentleman?"

"Spam for me too." Luca doesn't put on an accent.

"Excellent choice, sir!" Jake hands him a sandwich with another flourish. I smile at Jake; it's good to see him like this, seeming more like the old him, the one from before his parents' deaths.

Jake sits down with us and tucks into his sandwich. Adopting a French accent, he exclaims, "Thees is magnifique!"

I eat mine fast because I know that if I don't, my gag reflex will kick in. Once I've finished I swallow a gulp of water and whip out toothpaste from my pocket, pop a pea-sized blob on my tongue, and then hand to each of the boys. I'm sure I've had Spam before the invasion and I didn't mind it, but this Spam, this set-ration Spam, is slimy and gets stuck to the back of your throat. The only time it ever tastes nice is when Mena turns it into a hash.

"After dinner mints as well!" Jake drawls, and I laugh at him.

"Remember when you got thrown out of French because you kept speaking in a German accent and Mr Miller just lost it?"

"Mais monsieur, quel est le problème?" Jake repeats his performance expertly.

"He went purple!" Jake and I are laughing and I feel like it is the greatest victory to hear his joy and to actually feel that he means it.

"Remember when you saw Luca for the first time outside French and you nearly fainted?"

"Jake! I did not!"

"You did too; you went all breathy: *'Jake, who is thaaaaaat?'*"

"Ohmygod, Luc, I swear I didn't! Jake!" Admittedly, when I first saw Luca I was fifteen; he'd just joined the year above and he was this ridiculously gorgeous boy — it was hard not to be stopped in my tracks. But I did not say what Jake said.

"Was I wearing shorts?" asked Luca. "Shorts always get the ladies going."

I let out a surprised snort; Luca doesn't normally join in with this sort of banter.

"Yes, it was definitely some form of sports kit," Jake responded knowingly.

"Well, *you* were clearly paying attention." I elbow Jake in the ribs.

Jake turns his voice saccharine. "Look at the man, who wouldn't. *Those muscles.*"

Luca turns away embarrassed, never enjoying being centre of attention.

"Let's get back to work." Luca stands up and begins pushing the cart.

"Oh, just look at the way his muscles flex when he pushes. Golly!"

I elbow Jake again and snigger like an idiotic schoolgirl. I know Luca probably hates us right now but I am too happy to stop — Jake is being Jake again.

As we walk along laughing and teasing, Jake pulls me into a side hug and tugs my ponytail. My heart skitters. Things are definitely looking up.

At the end of my shift I begin thinking how I am going to get the drugs my mum needs; the obvious solution is to get sent to the work camps by Sesellend. I figure the best way for me to get into trouble is for me to achieve something whilst doing it. Jake and Emma's old home has become a kind of military building and there is something inside that I know they both want.

At 8:30pm that same evening I creep down the alley that runs parallel to their house. At 9pm the soldiers leave for patrol, which means I don't have a lot of time before the soldiers coming off duty show up. Climbing over the back fence I push open the kitchen window. I pause, crouching in the sink listening for any noise, and then carefully climb down. The place is littered with beer bottles, poker chips, and cigarette butts. Quietly I make my way upstairs to Jake's parents' old bedroom — the room where they had died. I hold my breath as I approach the door, my hands trembling. Carefully I push the door open; I don't know what I am expecting; blood, I suppose. There is no one inside and so I make my way to the wardrobe. I feel around on the top shelf until I find it, a small tin

Jake had shown me once. I put it into my backpack and take Julia's disregarded perfume bottle from her dressing table; Emma will appreciate it. Feeling bold now, I make my way into Emma's room but I can't see anything she'd really want that is worth the risk of being caught. In Jake's room I lose focus; it still smells like him. Not much of his stuff is left but it still sends me back to the times I'd sat on his bed with him talking about stupid things, him holding court, as always, making me laugh, making the world so much better for him being in it. I wish the GDO would leave just so we could sit on his bed again.

The sound of the front door opening returns me sharply to reality. I go back into Emma's room, open the window, and look down. The wheelie bin is still there; I let out a sigh of relief and climb over the windowsill. Bracing myself for the fall and for getting caught, I jump. The crash is louder than I expect; now that the streets are silent at night you can't muffle even the slightest of sounds.

My ankle hurts but I don't care, I just run. I know the streets better than the soldiers do, so I can get lost in them easily. Near the Kemeis' I slow down and allow my breath to come back. I check my watch: it's 9:20pm and the local patrol will come past soon; it's perfect timing. I step out onto the main street.

"What are you doing out past curfew?" A young soldier stands in front of me.

"I lost track of time, I was just helping a friend. I'm sorry, sir." I bite my lip in false shame.

"Name?" He stands to attention.

"Cassia Fortis."

"Work number?"

"46542."

"You will be punished for this infraction." The soldier is nervous; he's clearly new to the job. I don't want him to put me down as a suspected dissident — that would mean prison time.

"Sir, please, I didn't mean to." I make myself sound scared; I want him to think he has intimidated me.

"Law's the law... but I'll put it down as a minor violation."

I give him a sheepish smile. "I won't do it again, I promise. Thank you sooo much."

He smiles awkwardly at me, just like any other guy.

With my heart pounding, I enter the Kemeis' home. I am wiping the sweat from my face with my jumper as Luca walks in. He looks at me as though he knows everything that's just happened. I smile at him and shrug; he just shakes his head and walks into his room.

WEEK TWO

As I am pulling on my overalls on Monday morning, a soldier truck arrives; Luca shoots me a loaded look.

"Hey, Jake, can I borrow your backpack?"

"Um, yeah… why?" Jake tosses it over to me.

"It's bigger than mine." I quickly pass my bag over to him before the soldiers approach. "Oh, and you might want to take a look inside."

Jake looks puzzled and a little wary but there is no time to explain. "Is it safe to open?"

I smile mischievously back at him and then turn to face the two soldiers approaching.

"Cassia, what's going on?" I can hear the worry in Jake's voice.

"Just off to work the fields for a few days, nothing to worry about."

Luca lets out a low cough. Ignoring him, I walk towards the soldiers. They nod at me and lead me to the back of the truck. I climb in — there are three people already inside; a man in his fifties who smells of stale alcohol and vomit, a man in his twenties who looks extremely angry, and a pretty blonde who is about my age. I sit down next to her and introduce myself.

"Yve." She smiles back and shakes my hand.

"What you in for?"

"I spat in a soldier's meal because he pinched my arse. It was worth it. You?"

I like her attitude.

"Out after curfew," I shrug, like it's no big deal, even though I am new at this rebellious thing.

"Been there." There's a glint in her eye.

After picking up a few more people we arrive at the fields just after nine. It's spring so the air is warm and the sun is out, a perfect day to work outside. Yve and I are put on the same team, along with four others. We're sent to a field that's about ten minutes' walk away from the main base, and each team is allocated their own guard. After our instructions we set to work, but every chance I get I'm examining our surroundings. The border runs alongside the base, and there is a wire fence topped with barbed wire. Not far from the guarded border entry there's a row of bushes — the perfect access point. Beyond that, the river — helpfully it has a bridge — and then more fields; the crops are low so I will have to crawl until I reach the small wooded area in the distance, and beyond that is Sesellend and the medical storage facility.

At eight o'clock there isn't enough light to work, so we're escorted back to our living quarters. Dinner is watery soup, and then on to the shower block. My clothes have stuck to me with sweat, my back and legs ache, and my ankle throbs. I get into the shower fully clothed, not caring that the water is warm, not hot. I soap my clothes, and then my skin and hair. I dress in the clothes I'm given, rolling the trousers up five times and the shirtsleeves three times, looking like I've dressed in my dad's clothes. When I leave the shower block Yve laughs at me.

"You look ridiculous." Somehow she pulls off the work attire; I guess tall blondes can do that.

"The GDO clearly doesn't like short people." I look down at my outfit and laugh at myself.

"I don't think they like anyone." Yve's accent doesn't sound local, it's near perfect, but there is a hint of something different in there.

"You from here or were you a refugee?"

"Refugee. Came here three years ago with my mum." She is matter of fact, like she's telling me she'd just moved house, like people did before the war.

"I'm sorry." And I mean it; being a refugee means that she will have lost her home, loved ones, everything.

Yve shrugs. "We're all in this together, in a way that's a comfort."

"Not really. There isn't much to hope for any more." I look around at our prison.

Yve smiles. "Oh, there's always something."

I study her closely. "You're up to something."

"Me? Not at all, but *you* are and I want in." I am surprised by her perceptiveness but grateful I don't have to ask her for help. I smile in response.

"I have no idea what you're talking about."

A soldier approaches and shows us to our bunks. Yve and I decide to share — she gets the top. Once the soldier leaves she hangs her head over the side and in a serious voice says, "We'll discuss this tomorrow." I laugh and agree.

I sleep deeply thanks to the previous day's labour. We are woken at 6am, fed, and sent to work. Aside from the fields my day isn't much different to that in the city. At 10am we are given a water break and I take the opportunity to ask our guard how long our stay will be. I'm told we'd be leaving Sunday morning, which means I only have a few days to get to Sesellend.

Yve and I begin work at the far end of the field; it is our first opportunity to speak freely.

"I want in."

"It's dangerous... I can't ask you to help me." I squint into the sunlight to make sure our guard isn't approaching.

"You're not asking, I'm telling. I'm in. I want to help — I want to do *something*." She is stubborn, possibly even more stubborn than I am, and I trust her instinctively. I learnt from the war that you need to be cautious with trust, but my new rebellious nature doesn't like caution so I go with my gut and it tells me Yve is with me all the way.

"Okay. I'm going to steal medical supplies, here's what I'm thinking: our best bet is to go at night, wait for everyone in the camp to fall asleep, and we make it to the fence over there." I nod in the direction of the bushes. "We'll have to make a run for it across the bridge — we'll be exposed — and then we crawl to the woods through the fields, and on the other side is Sesellend. I checked an old map book, the medical facility is really close, just two buildings to the right of the main road into the town."

"How will we get in?" Yve bends down as the guard looks over. We go back to work as we talk.

"I was thinking an old-fashioned smash and grab?"

Yve smiles. "Well, if that's not possible I think I have some skills I can bring to the table."

She says it casually, not trying to brag.

"Like what?"

"Let's just say this isn't my first break in." I shake my head in disbelief. I really did stumble across a great partner in crime.

That night we pay attention to the guard's evening habits. Drinking, card games, and falling asleep in their chairs seem to be standard practice. Only one guard takes his job seriously; he is a potential problem.

The following day we collect the few supplies we'd need. Every evening we have to clean up the barn where everything is stored. Yve finds a nail in an old wooden plank and had two kirby grips in her hair when she'd been picked up, which are perfect for lock picking. I manage to unearth some rusty pliers buried at the back of the barn under some straw. Luck is on our side.

Yve and I agree we'll test to see how easy it is to get out at night. As this is my plan I insist on doing the test. Around 12am the guards are all snoring, except for the jobsworth who is awake and alert. When he gets up to walk around the block, I take my chance and hop out of bed, making my way past the sleeping soldiers. Outside I can see the soldier walking a circuit of the area. Keeping to the shadows I make my way towards the shower block and once there I will be hidden from view as I make my way towards the fence. A hand grabs my right shoulder; terrified, I spin around and stare back at the guard. I thought he was around the other side of the building.

"Jeez, you scared the crap out of me!" I pull my arm from his grip in irritation.

"What do you think you're doing?!" He tries to stare me down.

"I needed to pee!" I make myself look as indignant as possible.

"You can't just wander out at night."

"Everyone was asleep and I'm desperate. This isn't a prison you know; I can pee if I want to."

He grabs my hand and twists it upwards and back.

"Ow! What are you doing?"

He walks me backwards until I am against the wall and then, using his other hand, he squeezes my neck. I'm not being strangled but it isn't far off.

"S-s-stop," I manage to choke out, as the panic rises up within me.

"This isn't summer camp little girl. Take your piss and then get back to your room."

"Yes, sir."

I go into the shower block, desperately trying to hold back the tears.

Disappointed and scared, although I wouldn't admit that to anyone, the next day Yve and I try to think what else we could do; we can't leave much later than midnight, as it would take us a while to get there and back. I am frustrated and my back is aching. Jonas, a fifteen-year-old pain-in-the-arse, is trying to flirt with Yve on our way back to camp. Showing off, he decides to trip me and I fall into a puddle of mud. His mistake; him tripping me reminds me how a group of girls taunted me on a camping trip when I was ten. I decide I will get revenge the old-fashioned way. And it will help us break out.

The next few days Yve and I can't stay awake; our work is exhausting us and we're not used to such hard labour. We have missed too many opportunities. Before we know it, it's Saturday night and our last chance to get to Sesellend. The adrenalin keeps us wide awake that night. At 1am the vigilant guard takes his walk around; I creep to Jonas' bed and put his pinky finger into my warm glass of water. At supper Yve had sat with Jonas and had kept filling his water glass as she chatted to him, and he had about two pints inside him. The prank works quickly and Jonas wakes up soon after; horrified, he gathers up his sheets whilst Yve and I try not to laugh. He runs out of the room, with his urine-soaked sheets under one arm, and nearly bumps into the guard. We watch as he is escorted to the shower block to clean up.

We stuff our duvets with pillows and clothes and sneak outside, with the drugs list carefully zipped into my cargo work trousers. The guard is standing outside the shower block so we make our way to the left of the building and wait. Shortly afterwards we hear the guard and Jonas re-enter the building, then walk quietly to the back of the shower block. With our path clear, Yve turns to me and winks. I smile; going against the GDO is pretty exhilarating.

The pliers are badly rusted so it takes us longer than we want to make a big enough hole in the fence. We manage to edge through safely and right in front of us, the bridge arches over the water to Sesellend. We check and double–check, and then run harder and faster than I thought I could, until we reach the fields where we lie down on our bellies and begin our long army crawl. After what feels like hours we make it to the trees. On the edge of the town we pause. The streetlights are going to be a problem; there's clearly a curfew in place in Sesellend as well. We can see the medical storage building on our right with only one guard on duty, tantalisingly close. A security alarm box is attached to the wall and blinks in warning. I nudge Yve who just nods. She'll deal with it.

We wrap our jumpers around our heads to disguise our faces from any cameras on the streets, and we approach the building. I pick up a stone from the ground and throw it high so it bounces off the corrugated roof of the adjacent building — turns out javelin throwing was good for something after all. Suddenly the guard is alert; his gun is up and trained on the roof. He makes his way towards the source of the noise, clearing our path to the building. We find the back door and Yve gets to work on the keypad next to it. Using the pliers, she pulls off the front cover to expose the wires, and using the nail we'd found shorts the circuit. The door clicks and we enter.

Inside there's a long corridor with doors either side. We look through the glass windows but can see only labs; I feel myself start to panic. What if the medicines aren't even here? We keep going but I'm getting increasingly anxious. We reach the very end of the corridor and discover the storage warehouse. Using the two hairpins, Yve unpicks the lock. Inside there are rows of shelves with labelled blue boxes. We make our way systematically down the aisles collecting half their stock of each medication, in the hope that the break in won't be noticed immediately.

I search until I find what I'm looking for — Imatinib. There are six bottles, and I take all of them. Yve approaches and looks at me sympathetically; gently she puts two bottles back. She rests her hand on my shoulder; I know she's right, but it stings. All I want is for Mum to get better but Yve is risking everything to help me, so I swallow my annoyance and we move on.

We check the room for any signs of our presence and then shut the door carefully behind us. Outside Yve is re-attaching the cover to the keypad when we hear footsteps. The guard is coming. We can't run; all the pills in our bags would rattle like maracas and bring every guard in the area straight to us. Instead, we crouch behind a wheel of a nearby van. We hold our breath as the guard makes a circuit of the building. He passes the back door without noticing anything. As he rounds the corner we slip back into the safety of the woods. When we're about five trees deep, we hear the clatter of metal. The cover has fallen off the security pad, and the guard runs back to where we were only moments before. Yve reaches for my hand and squeezes it. Fighting our instinct to run we walk back through the woods. We keep at the same pace, being careful where we tread, our hands firmly clasped together in fear. At the clearing we look back and make out the faint blinking of torches.

We lie down and breathe in the scent of the fresh earth; the dew on the crops is refreshing at first, but gradually begins to soak through our clothes as we crawl through them. We can sense the guards getting closer but we carry on — the fence is in sight.

Finally, we reach the fence and crawl through. It's 5:15am, it's getting lighter, and everyone gets woken up at 5:30am. The guards could already be awake. The coast is clear and so I pull my backpack onto my front and hug it to my chest. Yve follows my example and we hurry towards the shower block — our bags rattle but not as much as they would have done. We have just reached the main building when we hear voices from the border and a figure begins to move through the shadowed approach towards the base. We freeze in place hearing talking inside and see the strict guard heading out with another soldier, towards the figure in shadow.

I mouth, "Now or never," to Yve. We slip inside the base. The other guards are still snoring soundly. We make it back to our beds, stow our bags under our bunk, and strip off our wet clothes. Yve climbs up into bed and I crawl into mine. Seconds later the guard enters and yells for us all to get up for a roll call. I quickly pull on a long t-shirt but Yve just climbs down in her underwear. We all stand in a line, the guard and soldier finding it hard not to stare at Yve. When they turn to talk to each other, Yve discreetly brushes her thumb behind my ear, and as I look at her perplexed she opens her hand to show a smear of mud. I try to steady my breathing. Our guard turns back to us and orders us all to get ready; we'll be heading back to town in thirty minutes.

Relieved, Yve and I pack up all our things, including our wet clothes. We file into the back of the truck and carefully stow our rucksacks underneath our legs. I keep telling myself we haven't got away with it yet; I need to stay alert. After five minutes, I'm fast asleep.

Yve wakes me up to say goodbye and that she'll see me around. They drop me at the Kemeis' but instead of going inside, I make my way straight to the hospital to see Mum. Once there I go to Dr McMawny's office, open up my backpack for him, and let him look inside. His eyes widen.

"Thank you." I can see that he understands how I come to have most of the drugs on his list but I also know he won't tell a soul.

"Just save my mum, okay?"

"I'll do whatever I can but I can't make any promises."

I sigh; even with the right medication she may not live, I know that.

"Thank you for everything you do for her." I smile at him and help him unload the drugs. "Oh, and Dr McMawny, a friend of mine will be coming to see you. You'll want to meet with her." He nods in bewilderment.

I make my way down the familiar hallways, my step a little lighter, and turn onto my mum's ward. When she sees me coming she looks at me with so much love and joy and I know that the risk was worth it. My mum deserves to live and she deserves to live in a free nation. We all do.

WEEK THREE

I wake up excited that I'll be seeing Jake again, that I only have to clean streets and not work in the fields. As Luca and I walk down the dimly lit streets, I hum to myself. He gives me a friendly elbow.

"What's got into you?" There's a smile in his voice.

"Nothing." I can't hide my joy; it's bubbling out of me. I haven't felt this way in a long time.

"You're up to something."

"I'm not, I swear."

His dark eyes study me.

"There's an aura of trouble about you."

I laugh and it feels natural, not like the laughing I'd been doing recently. It's the laugh of someone who feels hope.

"Hasn't there always been?"

He turns to me, serious, deadly serious. "Cassia, whatever you're up to — just stop, okay? It's not safe to be acting out; you could get in serious trouble, or worse." His brow is creased with concern.

"Luca, first of all, 'acting out'? I'm not two. You're not my dad. And, secondly, I don't know what you're talking about." My step is still light.

"No?" He looks around with caution. "What about the stuff you stole from Jake's old house?"

I sigh. "He lost his parents; I wanted to do something nice."

Luca should have known that.

"Anyway, I didn't get caught, well, not really. Work camps aren't so bad you know."

"I was watching out the window that night because I was worried. I saw you — you got caught deliberately. What are you really up to?" He stops in front of me, forcing eye contact.

"Nothing. Lighten up! It's a beautiful day."

He looks up at the slate grey sky and sighs. "Just promise me one thing: next time you have a scheme, let me in on it."

I look at him in surprise.

"At least then I might be able to stop you getting into serious trouble."

I squeeze him affectionately. "Thanks, Luc. Hey, I met someone I think you might like."

He takes the bait, happy for our difficult conversation to be over. "Oh yeah?"

"Blonde, 5' 8", and possibly far more stubborn than me."

He grins at me. "I don't think I could handle anyone who is as stubborn as you, let alone more so."

His posture begins to relax, thankfully. I don't need him protecting me.

"You'll meet her soon and then you can make your mind up."

When we reach the store Jake is already there, one foot in his overalls. He turns when he hears us approaching and runs up to me, picks me up, and twirls me around. He puts me down and then pulls me into a warm, tight hug.

"Thank you, Cassia, thank you." He looks at me. "You shouldn't have taken that risk for us but I can't thank you enough. We didn't have any pictures of them and, well… I'm so sorry you got into trouble for it. Oh, and Emma loves having Mum's perfume, she's sprayed it onto her pillow, she says it's like having Mum there when she shuts her eyes."

Tears glisten in his eyes and he coughs to cover them. "Anyway, I owe you, it was a really nice thing to do, you're the best friend in the world."

I'm crushed but I try not to show it. Out of the corner of my eye I see Luca looking at me sympathetically. For some reason this annoys me.

"Hey, you'd have done it for me." I brush it off, like it's no big thing, even though, to me, he's everything.

"I dunno, dunno if I'm brave enough to break into a house full of Crones."

When the war reached us we called anyone who joined up with the GDO "Cronies" because they were the GDO's best buddies, doing everything they were told no matter how idiotic. It was a childish name to try and make it feel like less of a betrayal, because when your own people abandon you and join up with the enemy, there isn't really a great way to deal with it. Recently we'd started calling all GDO soldiers Crones.

"No one was home; it was a piece of cake." I start to pull on my overalls.

"How was labour camp?"

"Alright — pretty sure I've gained some muscles." I inspect my own arm.

"In a week?! I don't think so." Jake prods my bicep.

"I could take you."

Jake turns to Luca and chuckles. Luca is in his gear and ready to go; he just raises one eyebrow at me.

"Oh, and I made a friend there."

"Yeah?" Jake sounds sceptical.

"Yeah!" I bash my cart into him lightly. "I'm really easy to get along with."

A look passes between Jake and Luca. I roll my eyes and push my cart down the road; it's going to be another one of *those* days.

Nowadays you can't really socialise; no sleepovers, no trips to the cinema or meals out. There isn't much you can do when you are forced to work and you have a 9pm curfew. However, on Wednesday the GDO were putting on a football match, some sort of morale thing for us, and we could all attend. I have no interest in football but it means a half-day off work and hanging out with my friends, which meant Jake, so I'm looking forward to it.

Luca and I wait outside the main stadium for Jake and I'm hoping to catch Yve on her way in to introduce her to Luca. Jake and Emma came together and I convince them all to wait five more minutes to see if my "fictional friend" (as Jake's calling her) would show up. I shouldn't have worried about trying to spot her in a crowd; Yve is hard to miss. When she sees me she runs up and we hug each other tightly, grinning at each other, sharing in our little triumph.

"Did you hear about the raid on the GDO's arms storage, here in Amphora, last night?"

"No…" I hope Yve isn't trying to tell me she was part of the scheme because if she was I'd helped to create a full-blown rebel.

"They're saying it's the Resistance," she whispers with so much excitement I'm pretty sure other people can hear.

"There's no such thing."

Her eyes widen with incredulity; in her mind of *course* there is. As we head into the stadium I notice Jake staring at Yve. I can feel a bad mood coming on.

Inside, the stadium is packed; it's the first time in ages that I have the feeling of being part of something. We sit in a block, with Luca and Jake behind Emma, Yve, and I. The two teams, made up of soldiers from two different GDO regiments, make their way onto the pitch. The crowd roars and I can't help feeling uplifted. There's no anthem played; the players just take their places and the game begins. Emma, Yve, and I laugh and chat our way through the first half, which means we have to ask the boys who's winning.

At half-time we go to get drinks. Jake is teasing Yve, which makes me uncomfortable, and Luca gives me a sympathetic look again. I pinch the back of his arm to make him stop.

"You're like a little wasp." He swats me away.

I stand on my tiptoes in response. "Don't call me little!"

"But you are."

I pinch him again and so he picks me up and threatens to drop me. I wriggle around him until I'm hanging my arms around his neck. Emma is laughing at us and so we continue to play fight, just to see her smile. When half-time is nearly over we head back to our seats and begrudgingly I let Yve and Jake sit together. As soon as the game starts again, the cheering picks up. It's so deafening that I can't hear anything Emma or Luca is saying. Five minutes in, over to the east, a plane approaches. There's a momentary silence, a collective intake of breath, of *knowing,* and then the billboards flash with a message:

GDO HAS ZERO TOLERANCE FOR
INSURGENTS.
ALL THREATS WILL BE ABOLISHED.

There's a deep booming sound, a sound that we all recognise.

Disasters happen in slow motion. The plane passes, the smoke billows, part of the stadium begins to crumble, and a scream rises, as one, from the lips of everyone within the stadium. People start to panic and stampede towards the exits. The ground is shaking from the blast and from the feet of thousands of people running in fear. Emma, Yve, and Jake turn to run but Luca and I stop them.

"We'll be trampled!" Luca helps Yve climb down to where we were standing and Jake joins us. We crouch down with our backs to the seats in front; Emma crawls into Jake's arms, shaking and crying, whilst we all wait for the storm to pass. Dust blows around us and clings to every inch of us. It's in my eyes, my mouth; it's the taste, the sight, of destruction and fear. An eerie hush eventually settles over the stadium, and all we can hear is the ringing, our ears still vibrating from the after effects.

I feel too shocked, too disorientated to raise my head and take in the scene — Luca is the first to look around. Seeing him stand gives me purpose and I rise into the cloud of dust; there's blood on the floor, which I can't understand. As we approach one of the exits there are five people lying on the ground. One of them is Mr Granger, mine and Jake's form tutor. He'd always been kind. He'd let us leave for lunch early so we were at the front of the queue, and he was funny. His visionless, glassy blue eyes stare back at me. I kneel down just to be sure — there isn't a pulse, there is no breath. I sense someone behind me and look up into Jake's tormented eyes.

Mr Granger, like everyone else, looks as though he has been beaten up. Shaking, I reach across and take the pulse of the person closest to Mr Granger. Nothing. Yve steps forward as does Luca, and we check the other four. They are all dead.

Jake carries Emma out, shielding her eyes. As we reach the main exit there are more bodies, more than I can accept, and blood, so much blood. My body freezes; I can't understand what I'm seeing. How can this have happened just from people running in a panic? With his hand visibly trembling, Luca bends down and checks for life. Jake holds Emma to him tightly and takes her outside the stadium. Yve, Luca, and I check to see if anyone is still alive. I'm only able to continue by focusing my attention on not throwing up. I can't disrespect these people.

Only one man is still breathing. Yve and Luca help him to stand.

Luca takes control. "Cass, we'll take him to the hospital, you help Jake look after Emma."

I agree; I just want to be away from the horror around me.

Jake, Emma, and I walk back in silence to the flat they share with another family. We take Emma into their room and tuck her into her bed. I sing the song her mum used to sing to her until she finally falls asleep.

> *When the wind blows*
> *My Child, My Child*
> *I'll be back home*
> *My Child, My Child*
>
> *In all of the earth*
> *Forever will be*
> *The spirit of life*
> *And the essence of me*
>
> *All that you want*
> *My Child, My Child*
> *Will surely be*
> *My Child, My Child*

The words of the song taste bitter in my mouth. I'd never realised how sad the old lullaby was and I regret singing it. But it soothes Emma, and I watch the tears dry up slowly on her cheeks.

I join Jake back in the family room. My mind is still whirling with thoughts of "all that you want... will surely be". His fists are clenched and white when I walk in. In a hoarse whisper he exclaims, "How could they do that?! I can't believe they did that on purpose, putting on that stupid match so we could all watch them drop that bomb."

I hang my head, unable to watch his anger. "I know."

"You know, a few years ago, when I heard that they use terrorist tactics to keep people in line I didn't believe it. I thought, things are bad but they're not that bad. I was so naïve... My... my parents, and now *this*."

I look back at him and try to get him to calm down by softening my tone. "I know, Jake."

"STOP SAYING YOU KNOW!" Tears prick my eyes.

Jake runs his hands through his hair, trying to calm himself, "I'm sorry, Cass."

But I don't hear the apology in his voice. He turns back to me and takes both my hands and says it again, and I can feel the warmth of his sincerity. He pulls me close and wraps his arms around me and then, before I know it, his lips are there and then he's kissing me. Jake kissing me — it was all I could think about for the past four years. His kissing turns more urgent, more heated, and then I realise that he isn't kissing me for the right reasons, he's kissing me because he's angry at everything and his hatred is burning him up. I push him away; he looks at me, wounded.

"Jake, it's just that… just slow down, okay?"

He turns his back on me.

"Whatever, Cassia."

I put my arms around his waist. He lets out a sigh, then removes my hands and walks away.

"I'll see you later."

He walks into the room he shares with Emma and I just stand there, wondering how I could have messed everything up so badly.

Out on the street there is the same eerie quiet that the war brought with it, but it's only 5:30pm, too early for so much silence. Everyone is in their homes, too afraid to come out. The GDO has achieved their goal; they've reignited fear into every citizen's heart.

Mena is making our rations into another inventive dish. She's humming to herself as she cooks; I stand and just watch her, until Luca comes up behind me.

"How does she do it?"

Luca rubs the back of his neck.

"She has faith that everything will get better." My heart sinks a little more; it doesn't feel much like things are ever going to get any better. I look up into Luca's big brown eyes, hoping to find comfort in his strength.

"I hope she's right."

"What's the matter? The football match?"

I shake my head. "Jake kissed me." I can't read Luca's expression.

"I thought that would make you happy?"

"So did I, but, I don't know. I guess… I guess war changes people," I pull my thin sleeves over my hands.

"Not everyone."

I look back at his warm face and allow myself a small smile.

"No, not everyone. Not you Luca, nothing could change you." I let him hug me and feel the calm he brings me. Always there, no matter what.

"Hey, how's that guy doing?" I look up at Luca, instantly regretting that I broke our hug.

"Doctor said they think it's just severe concussion, along with some scrapes and bruises," Luca pulls away and I feel cold, instantly.

"He was lucky. Do you see now?"

"See what?"

His expression is so serious that I instinctively hold my breath.

"Why you can't mess about stealing things? The GDO only sends you to work camps if you break small rules. If they catch you, I don't know, stealing medical supplies say…" I keep holding my breath. "… then the punishment would be much more severe." He glances up to the TV where the news is reporting the GDO's earlier triumph.

"What makes you think I stole medical supplies?"

"Because I *know* you, Cass."

I shake off his grip. "But don't you see, Luc? Don't you see that someone has to do something?"

"Let someone else do it." He is pleading with me.

I match his tone. "If everyone let someone else try and fix things, they would never get solved."

"I thought you might say something like that. I was hoping you wouldn't but I thought you might."

I risk a cheeky smile. "So, you really do know me."

He looks so sad that it almost makes me not want to go against his wishes. Almost.

"I meant what I said before; I'll help, just to stop you being reckless."

"I'm not planning on doing anything reckless."

Bringing Luca in on what I'd been thinking about scares me — he would be so angry if he knew. I know the risk I will be taking but I can't just let the GDO get away with keeping my dad prisoner. He's never harmed anyone or done anything remotely illegal. I want to free him, but how? The GDO is just too big.

That's when Luca nudges me.

"You know, I've been thinking about this a lot, and maybe I do want to do something too."

"Really?" I bite my lip in anticipation, not really believing him.

"And maybe we're thinking along the same lines." There's a spark of something new in Luca but I can't quite put my finger on what it is.

My dad once told me that knowledge is power. I know that this is something a lot of people say, but when he told me, it finally made sense to me. Knowledge *is* power. To challenge the GDO I am going to have to know everything about them. Only then will I know their weaknesses, and only then can I strike.

Luca and I don't go to work on Thursday morning; instead we head straight to our local barracks and enlist as Crones.

WEEK FOUR

Enlisting reminds me why I don't like the GDO —
so much paperwork and then medical exams and
the GDO's version of a background check, which
just means them pulling out a file that they already
have on you. It is a little frightening to see how
much they know. My small trip to the work camp
didn't exactly help matters, and neither did my
dad's political history but somehow, I'm still
allowed to enlist. Maybe they think seventeen-year-
olds are fickle.

    5am Monday morning and our training
begins. I decide not to tell my mum that I'm
joining up, but instead write her a letter explaining
I'm going to have to miss a few visits because I
have extra work duties. I hate lying to her but
neither do I want to put her at risk by telling her
my true motivations.

Luca and I are split up, as the women have separate dorms. There are three of us in a room that could sleep six; clearly, not many women are keen on becoming Crones. Esme and Camilla are my roommates; they aren't particularly chatty, although they seem pretty serious about joining the military. Outside in the yard we are made to line up in rows whilst we face inspection. I've managed to shorten my uniform over the weekend and so I'm well turned out. We each have the new type of waterproof backpacks that have the ability to float on water, which unnerves me — will they be dropping us in a large body of water and abandoning us in some kind of extreme survival experiment? We are then told we are heading out on a training exercise and I begin to feel very nervous. Since the war began, military initiation has become more of a "throw them in the deep end" approach. Two weeks of intensive training, then we'll be assigned to regiments, and the rest we will have to learn on the job.

Why we wanted to join was the first question they asked us when we signed up. I answered that I would feel safer in the army now that there are terrorists in our region. They took that as a good enough reason for a girl, despite her obvious past transgressions. Luca pulled off this patriotic routine; it was pretty impressive really. But standing among a group of recruits, I don't feel safer, I feel very, very exposed. Can they already tell that I am against them? Will they shoot me in the back in the forest and leave me for the wild animals? I have to pull myself together. It's then that I spot Luca; he looks the part, every inch a military man and handsome in his uniform. Seeing him makes me regain my focus. We have an objective.

At 6am our march begins. Monotonous, the only sound is the crunch of hundreds of boots marching in what should be unison, but it's more of a ragged line of misfits. At 12pm we're allowed a break, a drink of water, and some food. My feet are already burning and my shoulders are aching. Luca comes to find me.

"Let me take some of your stuff." He starts to unpack my bag.

"No way. If either of us get caught we'll be made to carry about five rucksacks." I stuff everything back in before anyone notices.

"True, but you look exhausted."

"I am; I don't have the build for this. How am I going to get through two weeks? Imagine if it was still a year's training." The thought actually makes me want to cry, which can only mean that I'm really, really tired already. Luca gives me a kind smile.

"I'll be right next to you the whole way. Don't worry, I won't let you fail."

I dig my fingers into his ribs as affectionate thanks.

As we continue our seemingly never-ending march, I'm thinking about Jake. I haven't seen him since we kissed; Luca and I decided the fewer people who knew what we were doing the better, and Jake isn't exactly acting calmly and rationally at the moment. I feel really bad that we haven't let him in on our plan. He'll be wondering where we are, and he'll be angry that I rejected his advances and then disappeared. I've made things so much worse and it keeps churning through my mind.

The light's fading and we are still marching. Luca is keeping in step with me but my body is turning to jelly, everything aches in a way I've never experienced before, and I just want to stop.

"Keep going," Luca whispers, sensing my exhaustion. "You can do this."

"I can't," I grumble back, but I keep going because he's right; I can do it, because I *have* to. Luca is risking everything as well; I can't let him down. We march until we reach a clearing in the forest at the base of the Adem mountain range. As soon as my rucksack slides from my shoulders, I feel like I could float to the top of the nearest peak. We are told to put up our tents and eat. Luca and I pitch next to each other. I can smell food, but I'm so tired I crawl into my tiny tent and fall asleep. Not long afterwards, I am nudged awake.

"Oh no, do we have to start marching again?"

Luca laughs at me. "No, but you need to eat otherwise you'll be wrecked tomorrow."

I grumble but I eat the unidentifiable stew and thank him.

"Turn round."

"Why?"

"Just do it, okay? You're going to be really sore tomorrow; I'm just going to rub your shoulders to help loosen them."

As if I can object to that. His hands are big and warm and I can feel the knots in my shoulders loosening easily under his touch. He orders me to turn back around so he can do my calves.

"Seriously? This is weird."

"Trust me, Cassia, you need this. Look at your puny legs. You are going to be sore but this will help." Relieved that I decided upon one last leg shave before training, I stick out my right leg.

"That feels so strange." My calf is tingly and sore and tickly all at the same time.

"Yeah, calf massages are."

I grimace but let him carry on. "How come you know this stuff?"

"Used to see a physio after training, just copying what they did." He concentrates on the massage, I think to avoid feeling embarrassed. Luca was always more reserved than me so it's strange having him help me in this way.

"Do you miss playing? You were good enough to make a career of it."

"If I could have, I would have, but things change. You just have to accept it and move on."

Sometimes I don't understand Luca. He's so accepting of everything even though, like the rest of us, all his dreams have been stolen.

"Do you believe in God?"

He looks at me, surprised by my sudden question.

"In a way."

That explains it; only religious people are so peaceful. I realise how hard joining the army is for him. He's a gentle giant. I just hope it won't break him.

"Okay, my turn to help you out."

"I'm fine, really."

"Shut up and turn around." I have to put my body weight behind my massage to make any kind of impact. "Your shoulders are like bricks! Do they hurt?"

"That's muscle Cassia, something you might have by the end of this."

I pummel his shoulders as revenge for his insult but he barely even notices.

"Fine, I give up."

Luca gets up to leave.

"Thanks Luc. Thanks for joining with me, for looking out for me. I couldn't do this without you."

"I know." He gives me his cheekiest grin and then makes his way outside. I fall asleep with a smile on my face.

I'm not smiling when we're woken up at 5am the following morning and have to pack our tents in near darkness.

"I think we're heading up there."

I follow Luca's gaze towards the mountaintops and let out a sigh. "Well, good thing I brought my personal physio with me."

"How you feeling?"

"Not as bad as I thought. I think that massage really helped. You?"

"Never better." He picks up my rucksack and straps me in; I let out an involuntary groan which makes Camilla smirk in my direction. I steel my gaze; I may be small but it doesn't mean I can't take her. Luca catches my scowl.

"You've got a mountain to climb, remember? Don't want you running out of energy, Scrappy."

"I haven't scrapped in years but I've still got it."

"I don't doubt it." Luca stretches out his neck and then the line starts moving.

The first half of the day isn't so bad despite my already aching body because it's still relatively flat. After lunch we begin to make our way up smaller, steep tracks, which are covered in scree with a sheer drop on one side. Luca has me lead so he can give me the odd nudge up difficult parts. My shoulders are in agony; my calves are burning with an intensity that surely means I'm never going to be able to walk again.

"Good thing I'm not afraid of heights." I stare down at the treetops below and enjoy the feeling of the wind cooling off the back of my neck. I turn to look at Luca who is uncharacteristically pale. "Luc?"

"Just keep moving, okay?"

"Okay. Want me to go in front?"

"No, it's better if I just focus on your back."

"Have you been staring at my arse this whole time?"

Luca lets out a low laugh that's part humour, part terror. "Helps me forget about how high up we are, didn't realise I had a problem with heights until now."

I smile — it's not often Luca shows a weakness — so I keep on moving; moving means Luca can't think too much about the sheer drop and hopefully that we'll reach the top soon so that I can collapse.

The climb becomes increasingly difficult the higher we get. My body hurts so much that I begin to grind my teeth. Then we reach a plateau where the people in front are beginning to set up camp; we've reached our destination. Luca and I camp in the centre of the plateau, where he probably feels safest. As I'm picking my way back from using the toilet pits, I look over at the remaining people snaking their way to camp. Luca is walking towards me with our food when I see someone slip. The person behind makes a grab for them but they're not quick enough. Luca turns to follow my gaze but instinctively I stop him, shielding his view with my hands as I watch the body fall against the rocks, break, and then plummet into the trees below.

My entire body begins to shake.

"What was it?" Luca's face is filled with concern.

"Someone fell Luc, someone fell."

The horror on his face reflects how I'm feeling.

Our lieutenant announces the death when everyone has reached the plateau. Gregory Hammond was twenty-one and had joined up with his brother. I can see his brother, Simon, in the distance staring out over the edge of the cliff. The camp is quiet after that.

Just before I go back to my tent Luca asks me why I'd shielded his eyes and I explain to him that when I could, I will protect him too, like he's protecting me. He hugs me in a way he hasn't before; maybe it's gratitude, I don't know. I'm too tired to figure it out.

The next three days are more of the same: march all day from dawn to dusk and at night slowly sob ourselves to sleep. On Saturday we're finally back in the forest at the foot of the mountain range. I never thought I'd be so relieved by a day's marching before but anything is better than the difficult terrain of the mountains. It was colder, the air was thinner, and every step was a burden. Down at sea level there is almost a spring in my step, but that could be because the colour sergeant gave us "hot shots" — a tincture of benzoin that's injected into our blisters, post drainage — the day before, which at the time had me screaming but it does mean I can walk again.

That night we camp in the middle of the woods. Luca and I have started pitching our tents so they touch. I'm convinced his body warmth seeps out and keeps me warmer in the cold mountain air. Jono wolf-whistles mockingly at us. We laugh it off but when he goes to get his food we move his pitch so the entrance is touching the entrance to Drummer's.

"Drummer, how many times have I told you to stop trying to get into my back door?!" Jono hollers.

"Jono, how many times have I told you I'm not interested, you're too effeminate for me?"

Jono rugby-tackles Drummer, offended that his best mate doesn't think he's masculine enough for him. From what I can tell, they'd joined up as soon as they arrived in Auria as refugees. By the way they behave it's almost as if they didn't feel like they had anything better to do.

That evening I sit with Simon whilst he's eating his meal. I don't say anything; I don't know what to say anyway. When we've both finished eating, I take his bowl to wash it up and he thanks me. I can tell he is thanking me for sitting with him too. Nothing can take his pain away but it doesn't help that he's so obviously lonely.

It's 6am on Sunday morning when we're woken up by our sergeant; 6am must be the equivalent to a lie-in when you're in the army.

"You lot stink so, being the nice man I am, I'm giving you some time to wash. Follow me." There are whoops from everyone – after marching for days without washing there's nothing we all want more.

Our sergeant leads us through the forest to a waterfall at the base of one of the mountains, with an azure blue pool.

"Wash away!" The sergeant doesn't wait, stripping off and diving straight in.

Luca whispers to me, "Should I have shielded your eyes then?"

"Yes! Definitely!"

We both laugh and then there were naked men everywhere. I put my head in my hands and groan.

"I'm in hell."

"Come on, there's some rocks over there, I'll make sure no one looks."

"That includes you!"

"Of course…"

I swipe at him but he ducks.

Crouching behind a cluster of boulders, I peel off my uniform and decide to keep my underwear on. Stealthily I make my way into the water and then call Luca.

"All clear!" He is already in his boxers and climbs up onto one of the rocks and bombs me. I haven't felt so carefree in a long time and it feels like forever since I've been clean. I swim back up to my uniform and scrub my top in the water.

"It won't dry very quickly."

"That's why I'm only doing the top. It stinks, I can't stand it anymore."

"You're definitely not a soldier yet then."

"Shuddup." I sent a spray of water his way.

"Watch it or I'll pick you up and throw you and every man here will see you in your underwear."

"I do *not* want that."

We stay in the water until we are told to get out. My top isn't too wet by that time, thanks to Luca wringing it out. I also force him to wash his.

As we walk back to camp I think about my mum all on her own on a Sunday, and the effects of the swim quickly wear off. I feel guilty but I can't let myself lose focus; there's too much at stake.

We are taught how to catch and skin a rabbit that afternoon, not to mention how to gut it (urgh) how to build a proper fire that wouldn't burn down the entire forest, how to use a plastic sheet for shelter instead of a tent (which fills me with dread) and some other field crafts. That night our lieutenant announces he's leaving, along with all the other fully trained soldiers and our food supplies. And our tents. I knew it. Using our maps and compasses in teams of six, with only laser guns for protection, we are to make it back to headquarters in three days wearing a tactical training vest that registers laser shots as "kills". As trainees we will be pursued by our colour sergeant, lieutenant and the other soldiers we've relied upon for guidance — I'm not exactly sure how we're going to stand a chance.

"We are your enemy from first light and we will hunt you. Your lasers have a short range and so if you want to shoot us, you'll have to get bloody close. Oh, and before you all get too excited," said the lieutenant holding up a rifle, "we'll all be firing at you with these." He shoots Drummer in the arm who yelps in pain. "Our rifles have also been fitted with rubber bullets *so that they hurt*. Wear your helmets at all times; one of these to the head could cause some damage."

"Wouldn't affect Drummer, nothin' in there!" Jono yells, a few people laughing along with him.

The lieutenant shoots Jono in the thigh in response, causing the entire camp to roar with laughter. "And wear a cup, because we know where your brains are."

Jono rolls around in indignant pain.

"The winning team gets a steak dinner." There are cheers from the crowd; our food has been pretty bad over the past week.

"Each team will get a number, that number will be programmed into your laser rifles so that we know which team has made a kill."

Jono and Drummer agree to join Luca and me, along with their new sidekick Mateo who barely understands anything we say. He laughs in response to most things though, so he's good for morale.

"We just need a sixth." Jono is cleaning his nails with a twig.

"What about Simon?" I look to Luca to see if he agrees, and can tell he does.

"Urgh, he'll be such a downer." Mateo, sensing Drummer was being funny, starts laughing.

"His brother *just* died. Besides, did you see the traps he made? They were really good; he could be the only reason we have food over the next three days."

Jono and Drummer let out a collective sigh and agree to Simon joining us. Luca and I offer

Simon a place on our team; he seems relieved that he hasn't been left out. With our group in place, all we have to do is get back to base. We collect our rifles and our number, Number 8.

WEEK FIVE

We're all up at 5am without needing an alarm, our bodies having finally adapted to our new routine. The absence of our lieutenant and the other soldiers can already be felt in the camps. It rained a little in the night and a lot of people had not bound their shelter sheets properly and so wake up pretty grumpy and resentful that their tents have gone. Drummer organises what rations we have for our breakfast whilst the rest of us quickly pack away our stuff. It's clear that his priority in life is always food and that the steak dinner is probably the greatest motivation he's ever been given. With our helmets on we begin on our way, taking it in turns to navigate; apart from Mateo who can't map-read and has no idea what the purpose of a compass is.

We want to keep at a good pace but we're aware that at any moment we could stumble into a trap. Mateo seems to have the lightest tread and Drummer's pretty sharp at spotting things. The rest of us keep in a loose formation behind them.

Two hours in, we hear a popping sound ahead. Drummer spots a soldier hiding in the trees. We all get down and let Drummer locate our 'enemy'. There are five in total, along with the injured team whose vests are lit up red to indicate they've been hit. Carefully we pick our way around their position, and continue.

We manage to get through the first day without being spotted by soldiers. We've seen a few groups as we've continued forward but we always make sure to split into smaller groups; twelve people are much easier to spot than six. For lunch I help Simon build rabbit traps, it's too risky having a fire at night. Mateo is pretty handy with a knife and skins and guts the rabbits with Jono's help.

That night Luca and I keep watch whilst the others relax under their shelters.

"We should have someone on watch all night." I am already starting to think like a soldier.

"I can take the first shift." Luca offers.

"Are you sure?"

"I'm not too tired. Today was a breeze compared to the mountains."

"You were *not* a fan of them."

Luca smiles. "Prefer my feet on solid ground."

I look down at his feet, "Wow, how big are your feet?! I've never noticed them before." I put my size four boots up against his.

"14. I'm a big guy." Luca flexes his arm muscles, which are triple the size of my thighs.

"Whatever." I roll my eyes at him. "Hey Luc, look, I'm getting some too." I roll up my sleeve and flex my right arm to show the beginnings of a muscle.

"We'll make a soldier of you yet, Cassia Fortis."

"Yeah, I can't wait."

Luca shoots me a sceptical look.

"I mean it, I don't want to feel like the weak one, I want to be able to hold my own."

"You can hold your own plenty."

The leftover rabbit isn't too bad and it helps me sleep. At 2am I am woken up by Simon to start my portion of the watch. The night is peaceful. Every so often my mind wanders back to my kiss with Jake and the more I think about it, the more I realise that kissing him has changed how I see him. He was my best friend but what I thought was there really isn't. Maybe it took that kiss to realise it, or maybe it's just the way war has changed us both.

I think about my mum and dad. How can I free my dad and reunite my parents? Sometimes everything feels just too big to solve, but my mum used to tell me to break things down when I became overwhelmed with schoolwork. So, I'll break this down. What do I want to achieve? First, I want my dad out of prison. He's in Camburg, a town forty-five minutes by car from Amphora. I want my mum better, but I've done all I can for her for the time being. And, like all Aurians, I want our country to be free again, but that goal is beyond me. Breaking things down doesn't make it any easier, but for now, my focus has to be my dad.

At 3am I wake Jono up and crawl into my sleeping bag to catch the last few hours of sleep.

We calculate that we will reach the edge of the forest by the end of the day, and that's when our cover will end. From there, it's open. We will have abandoned buildings to hide in but that's it. We decide we'll push on and find shelter in a building under the cover of darkness.

At lunch we decide to make another fire, although it's risky, so we can catch and cook enough food for the evening as well. All is quiet and we rest and eat without any interruptions. An hour into our post-lunch march, Drummer holds up his right hand to halt us. We all freeze. He indicates for us to get down, and we crouch down and wait. We hear the sound of a safety clicking off. We all instinctively look to Luca, who signals for us to scatter.

At close range, the firing of bullets makes a booming sound. In a flash I'm behind a tree, and Jono and Simon are crawling towards my position. Luca is behind a larger tree just along from me, with Drummer nearby. Mateo is making his way towards us silent as ever, when Luca signals something to him. Mateo salutes Luca and he begins running. Within a breath, he's out of sight.

We wait, keeping low, then Mateo appears behind a soldier to our left. Before the soldier can react, Mateo's shot him. The soldier's pack lights up red — he shakes his head mystified and smacks Mateo on the back in congratulations. He salutes and then vanishes again.

"Creepy little bugger."

I turn as Simon whispers. I smile at him, glad he's beginning to communicate more, even if I'm not sure if he's insulting Mateo.

A twig snaps a few feet up ahead and Luca signals for us to keep moving. Out of nowhere the crack of five, maybe six, guns breaks the still of the forest. Luca gestures for us to run right. We set off, running low, rubber bullets whipping past us. I don't think, I just run. Luca waits for Mateo and then together they set off in the same direction as us. When Luca catches up, he indicates that we should turn north, back on our original course. We run under the canopy of gunfire. After running for five minutes something catches Drummer's attention, and his eyes flick up ahead to the right. Luca follows his gaze and so do I; a gun is pointed directly at us. Then a click, a pop, and Luca's body is against mine. His weight slams me against a tree, winding me. Our breathing is heavy and his face inches from mine.

"You hit?"

He shakes his head, his face filled with concentration.

"Thanks." I manage to breathe again.

"No problem."

Jono lets out a barely audible wolf whistle but Luca and I simultaneously shoot him a withering look.

More bullets scream past us and we look to Mateo, the lone sniper blocking our path out of the forest. He nods and smiles, honoured to be our assassin. We lie waiting, my breathing still laboured but the pressure in my chest is starting to ease up. Luca asks me in a whisper if I am okay to run. I nod. I won't be a burden to my team. Mateo appears next to me, holding up his rifle and grinning widely. Our path is clear.

We set off at a sprint, our backpacks only slowing us down a little. I can't catch my breath properly and my body is still wrecked from days of marching but I keep pushing forward. We pass the 'shot' soldier who salutes Mateo as he runs past, and I can't help but smile. We have our very own stealth fighter. After about a mile Luca halts us, and we all catch our breath whilst Drummer does a quick scan. He nods. We're free and clear.

We start up at a marching pace again, my shoulders are killing, my feet have blisters again and there is sweat trickling down my back; I am going to stink the next day.

The light is fading fast when we reach the edge of the forest, and we can make out an abandoned barn a mile or so to the east. We rest and eat the remainder of the rabbit we've kept aside and when night finally descends, we begin carefully to make our way forward.

Jono and Simon lead the way as we approach the barn, the rest of us crouching low as they inspect the area. At the entrance, they stop and drop back. We stay still and listen. Inside we can hear men talking in low whispers. There's a window nearby so we peer inside. Our lieutenant is inside with eleven or so soldiers, one with his back to us — I'm sure he's the one Mateo shot last. We can barely make out what they're saying but they look settled in for the night. On Luca's command, we push on forward. In the distance we can make out a village. Keeping to the side of an old track, we approach cautiously. The closest building is an old church. Mateo scouts the area; there's no one around. The village, like most rural areas, is uninhabited — to keep an eye on the population the GDO moved people into towns and cities. Shells of houses sit lonely against the star-filled night; there's something melancholy about seeing places abandoned, as if the buildings miss being occupied.

The church is cool inside and smells of damp stone. I slip my pack from my shoulders and pull aside the red velvet curtain to find a small doorway. Behind the door is a small office with a bathroom off to one side. As I'm in a church I feel that praying is appropriate, and so I pray as I turn the tap. There's some spluttering rusty water at first but it soon runs clear. I thank the Lord, lock the door, and give myself a quick birdbath rinsing out my underwear and shirt. I pull my tank top and cargo trousers back on and rinse my socks out. There's a gentle knock on the door and Simon whispers through the door.

"What you up to in there?"

I open the door to him. "Just freshening up."

I'm hanging my laundry along the back of a pew when Jono approaches.

"Going commando?"

I ignore him — I'm going to be on the 4am shift so I settle down, using a hassock as a pillow. It's already midnight and I need some sleep.

Luca wakes me up by stroking my arm, then climbs into his sleeping bag when my eyes are open. I have goose bumps on my arm for what feels like half an hour after that. At least they keep me awake. The only sound I can hear is the gentle breathing of my teammates as they sleep. I stretch out my sore muscles and try to untangle my hair with my fingers and imagine how nice it will be to re-gain the frizz I hate from having clean hair. At 5am I wake the boys. They're quick to sort themselves out and we're back on our way by 5:20am.

Outside the sky is golden with the warm glow of morning as Drummer and Mateo take the lead. Unsure of who might be in the village, we keep to the outskirts where we're more visible but we can spot anyone nearby. We have calculated that we have fifteen miles to cover, which, if we keep a good pace, will take roughly six hours. Jono and Drummer point out that this will get us back to base in time for lunch. I am so sick of rabbit.

Barely a mile from the base there's a huge fence, topped with barbed wire and a sign warning of landmines.

"Seriously? This can't be right. Did they say anything about landmines?" Jono has become increasingly agitated the closer we get. He's probably thinking about a nice juicy steak, like we all are.

"Do we just go to the guards at the gate?" Simon gestures to one of the security posts. We watch as another group approach them, and the guards shake their heads. The team comes up to us.

"What did they say?" Drummer is restless, also desperate for his meal.

"We have to figure out our own way in."

A tall man in his twenties starts using clippers to cut a hole in the fence, and I smile in recollection. Luca gives me a look.

"What?"

"You look nostalgic."

"Pipe down."

We watch the first team make their way through.

Simon turns to us. "Should we follow them?"

"Something doesn't feel right; it was too easy. I think we should examine the perimeter."

Jono and Drummer roll their eyes at me.

"She has good instincts," said Luca, as always coming to my defence.

"Dude, look. They walk." Mateo gestures towards the other team crossing the grounds and then the earth shakes, my ears ring, and dirt and dust fly into the air. Ducking, we cough and splutter whilst the cloud passes. Then we hear the screaming. We stay down waiting for the dust to clear so we can assess what's happened. When the air is clear again we look across to where the group had been. One soldier is dragging his friend back to the fence — his friend, the man I saw cutting open the fence, is missing both his legs and is howling in an earth shattering way. There's chaos where the others are, the scene before us is horrific. A girl has lost her foot — as visibility improves I realise it's Camilla. I see what is left of her foot a few meters away. I feel sick. My heart pounds. There's no way, absolutely no way, that the GDO would let their own soldiers walk across an anti-personnel mine field.

But they did.

"I feel sick…" I crouch down and put my head between my legs, whilst the others just stand open-mouthed.

"How could they let that happen?" Simon's voice is shaking, as he gazes at the guards who are now calling in the explosion on their radios. They don't seem to care that six people have just walked across a mine field.

"We have to keep moving."

They all look down at me. I'm still crouching. The GDO soldiers at the gate begin to help the injured.

"We *have* to. It isn't safe for us to help them," callous, yes, but we could easily walk across a mine ourselves. I need to get away from the horror in front of us. I need to keep moving.

Reluctantly they agree, so together, we re-examine the map. I point to the barracks. "Here, this is where we get in." We begin walking automatically, a habit now. Over and over I keep thinking about those six innocent lives. How could the guards knowingly send trainees into a minefield? They've destroyed their lives. I'm so angry I could scream.

At the fence outside the barracks the boys look up, perplexed. I let out a frustrated sigh and hand Luca my backpack. I climb the fence and then tell him to throw me my bag when I'm near the top. I tie my bag lengthways along the barbed wire and climb over, jumping down onto the barracks' roof. The boys just look at me, confused. Come on, work it out! One by one, they climb over and jump down to join me. Luca is the last and he unstraps my bag and tosses it to me before jumping onto the roof. Drummer can't spot any snipers and so we drop down from the one-storey building and inch forward towards the exercise yard. There, in the middle, is the victory flag.

Luca looks at us. "As one?" We all agree and run to the centre; Simon grabs the flag and raises it above our heads. But we don't cheer; the game is over, but it doesn't feel like a victory.

Our captain approaches and shakes our hands in congratulations.

"You don't seem very thrilled. Odd. Usually the victors are begging for their steaks."

"Captain, team five, they… they tried to cross the minefield." Drummer runs his fingers through his sweat dampened hair.

"Ah, yes, I've just heard, very unfortunate. Sometimes these things happen, even in training. There are many casualties in war and it's a good lesson — there are no shortcuts." His tone is matter of fact, with not even a hint of remorse.

"Sir?" I hesitate — can you question your superior officer? "The war is over now though."

"Yes, absolutely, our job now is to keep the peace." He clasps his hands behind his back.

"So, those people who were hurt…"

"A tragedy, a real tragedy."

I stare at him in disbelief. He really doesn't care what happened. Is that the Crone way or is he just an uncaring person? The whole thing sickens me but strengthens my resolve. My dad needs to be away from these monsters.

"As you've demonstrated great teamwork you'll be assigned the same regiment, which means the same dorm. Ah …"

"Fortis," I offer.

"Fortis, will you need separate sleeping quarters?"

"Just somewhere I can shower in private." All the showers are communal; I'm not ready for that.

"Fine, that can be arranged." A cadet appears. "Cadet Ellison will show you the way."

I choose a bed in a corner next to Simon, in an attempt to stop Jono and Drummer teasing me about Luca, but everyone is subdued.

"You lot can shower first."

"You sure?" Luca, ever the gentleman.

"I can't stand the smell of you all any longer. Please, just wash."

He gives a small chuckle and Jono sniffs his armpits with glee.

"Fresh as a daisy — I don't think I need a shower."

"If you're in a bed next to me, you're showering," Drummer pushes Jono out the door.

I enjoy the chance to be alone; I'm never alone anymore. I unpack my bag, putting my dirty clothes in the laundry bag hanging off the end of my bed. Everything else is neatly organised in my bedside cabinet and my locker at the end of the room. We could get spot-checked at any moment, and it's not worth being put on cleaning duty; I've done enough cleaning for one lifetime.

I finally get my chance to shower when the boys return. I take the clean uniform from the end of my bed and the towel that has been laid out for me. My name is already embroidered onto the front of the uniform. I turn the water up so high that it's scalding my skin, soap my hair three times, and enjoy being able to shave my legs again. But the shower doesn't wash away the images that are plaguing me.

With my skin pink and glowing, I make my way back to our shared room. The boys are all scuffling on the floor.

"What's going on?" Luca is underneath Jono and Drummer, and he peers up at me. "They wanted to spy on you. I was trying to stop them!"

"Then why are you on the bottom?"

"They outnumbered me!" The boys free Luca and I scowl at them all.

"Shame on you. Drummer, really?" Mateo starts to giggle at "boobs". Drummer just shrugs; clearly he just wanted in on the fun. Boys.

I pull on my boots and we make our way to the mess. Steak, chips, and spinach is placed in front each of us. I can't help but salivate. The boys dig in straight away but I hesitate.

Luca is sitting next to me and speaks to me in a low voice, "What's the matter? You turned vegetarian all of a sudden?"

I respond in a whisper, "I just feel guilty."

"I know, but you can't think like that. You just have to think where all this will lead."

I still hesitate.

"It's really good. I bet you're starving."

"Fine." I take one bite and then I can't stop; it's the best food I've ever eaten, or in a long time anyway.

Our plates are cleared and then it's a large piece of chocolate fudge cake. My eyes practically fall out of my head; I haven't had chocolate in months. I haven't had cake in many, many months.

Luca grins at me and we all begin shovelling it in. The army has ruined my table manners.

Full and relaxed we sit back and watch the other teams file in. They're given a hearty stew that doesn't look too bad, but it's no steak. I smile at a few of them who I'd spoken with whilst we were out on exercise. I can see why people enjoy being in the army, there is a strong sense of solidarity between everyone in the room. But there's one empty table. Luca catches me looking and under the table he holds my hand. I can't help but wonder what else we'll lose along the way: fellow soldiers, family, friends.

We begin rifle training the next morning. None of my group have used a gun before so it's a pretty steep learning curve. By the end of the day my shoulder is badly bruised from the kick-back. The following day I'm shooting better. Drummer and Jono are good shots; Luca and Simon are the best. Mateo and I are definitely the bottom two of our group. Satisfied that we can all clean, assemble, point and shoot a gun, the next day we're given combat training.

I am terrible at combat training. Everyone is bigger than me and I keep getting the wind knocked out of me. Mateo is about the same size as me, but he's really quick and uses what looks like martial arts moves. Luca has his size as an advantage and he wins every fight. Jono and Drummer are dirty fighters; they use anything they can to bring an opponent down. They're both disqualified every time it's their turn, although they argue that in actual combat they can fight as dirty as they like. This gets them twenty laps of the yard. Simon seems to channel all his anger into his fighting, so he doesn't come off too badly.

At the end of the day I'm feeling pretty dejected.

"I sucked butt."

"Nicely put, Fortis," Drummer replies. We're cleaning our room, getting ready for an inspection.

"Mateo, how did you do all that stuff?"

"Huh?" Mateo's English isn't improving very fast. "I do karate chops." Mateo begins a series of very impressive moves.

"Seriously, is he a ninja? He can walk completely silently, kick the arse of men twice his size, and he appears out of thin air... a lot." I sit down on my bed to inspect my already badly bruised skin.

"Didn't you know?" Simon stops what he's doing and faces me.

"What?"

"He was some kind of martial arts master."

"Really?" Mateo is still doing his moves.

"Brought his family here just before it all went to hell, took him six months to get them across."

"How'd you know all this?" Jono asks.

"I asked him."

We all look at each other, perplexed.

"You speak…?"

"Portuguese. I was studying languages — Spanish and Portuguese. Also, a little French."

Luca looks at Simon. "Wow, we really don't know anything about each other."

"So, where are Mateo's family now?" I look at Mateo who has stopped moving and is grinning.

"When their refugee camp turned to slums he realised the only way to save his family was to join the army, where they'd be given family accommodation when he completed the training."

Mateo has done what he can to save his family but it meant joining the GDO. I know he's just trying to be a good husband and father, but it can't have been an easy decision. He is a good man, and we didn't even know it because we never even asked.

We get to know each other better that night. Jono and Drummer were farmhands on the Celtic hills. They had travelled across the channel waters and active war zones to make it to the last free nation after everyone they knew was lost to them.

When they finally arrived Auria was occupied but at least the war was over.

"Jono couldn't bear to leave his beloved sheep behind. They were his first lovers."

"Don't you mean loves?" Simon asks.

"No, lovers. Jono conformed to a stereotype. He really enjoyed being a sheep farmer. Really, really."

Jono just snorts, not bothering to rise to Drummer's bait.

They'd joined the army because they thought it'd be fun, now that the war was over. Just lots of marching and camaraderie.

Simon had joined with his brother, both looking for a career, and since the army was the best option available in such times, they'd signed up. It wasn't noble, I knew that, but I can't hold it against them. Everyone has their reasons. Very few seemed to want to join in with the Crone's cause, from what I could tell anyway.

Luca, I already knew, had come from Africa with his family when he was a child; war was a constant companion to his home nation. They all spoke perfect English and his father was able to get a job at our university. His mother was a poet, but she only ever wrote in their native language. She said there was more poetry in her mother tongue than any other.

I am the only one who was born here in Amphora, but we were all nationless now.

The next morning, we stand in the yard and are given our new regiments; every group of six is to remain together. As the winning team we have the privilege of starting where we want to be posted. None of the others has a preference and so I take the opportunity to suggest Camburg. No one has any objections, although Luca gives me a long look. We're given the rest of the day off and I'm granted leave to see my mum.

As a soldier I can't walk around in civilian clothing. The GDO likes to see as many soldiers around cities as possible. They say it sends a message. It sends a message all right; it says that the people are living under tyranny.

My mum can't hide the shock on her face when I enter, and it hurts. She does her best to act normal and I'm comforted to see she has some colour back in her cheeks — hopefully the medication is working.

"Mum, I'm really sorry but I'm not going to be around for a while." I fiddle with the buttons on my uniform, terrified that she hates me now — or doesn't love me as much now that I'm one of them.

"Why not? They're not sending you to fight somewhere are they?" Her face is contorted with concern.

"No, there isn't any fighting any more — we're being sent to Camburg to join our regiment." I smile at her, hoping she'll understand.

"Your father." Her eyes widen, understanding. "Cassia, no, don't do this."

I kiss her cheek in farewell. "Do what, Mum? I have *no* idea what you're talking about." I stop at the door and turn back to her. "No matter what happens in life, there's always hope Mum. Always."

Reluctantly she nods her consent. I know she doesn't like it but I also know that she understands what I'm doing. That's all I want, for her to understand. I never want her to believe I'd turn my back on our family. There's no point in giving up on the life you want; she knows that better than anyone.

WEEK SIX

The sun has burnt away the early morning clouds by the time we arrive in Camburg on Monday. The town is a shell of its former self — empty buildings and hardly any people on the streets. The people here haven't left, I know that, but I don't want to think too much about what has caused the population to halve in less than a year. Camburg has some of the same beauty as Amphora but the brickwork is different; most of the stones are grey, giving the town an even bleaker feel than it's already giving off. I visited Camburg few times when I was younger to see my great-aunt, and remember the streets bustling with a Sunday market, bright fruits and vegetables gleaming in the sun. It didn't seem so austere back then.

We are to report to the base, which was once the police headquarters adjacent to the prison; it's the first time I have set eyes on the walls that hold my dad. I haven't been so close to him in months and my heart begins to beat faster; it's as though I can feel his presence. We report to our new captain, Captain Kohler, who has pale blue eyes, blonde hair, and a pockmarked jawline. He's striking, but I wouldn't go so far as to say he was handsome.

An old school has been converted into sleeping quarters; the five of us are still bunking together but at least each shower has its own separate cubicle. Mateo, his wife, two-year-old son, and baby girl are housed in a flat nearby. Through Simon he tells us that he has running water, a kitchen, and a separate room for the children. He has done what he had to for his family; I understand doing what needs to be done, even if it comes with the bitter taste of betrayal.

That afternoon we're given a written test to assess our individual skills. Afterwards we're taken on a proper tour of Camburg and meet a few more soldiers in our regiment. Most of them haven't been in the army long and no two people appear to be from the same country. We're a jumble of nationalities and inexperience. I wonder how on earth the GDO has managed to win such a huge war with such a mishmash of people.

Understanding this might help me figure out its flaws.

My bed is next to Luca's and that night, when I'm sure everyone is sleeping, I turn on my side and watch his body rising and falling with each breath. Somehow it comforts and sooths me to sleep. When I open my eyes the next morning, Luca's face is the first thing I see and a warm feeling spreads over me. I lay on my back and stare at the ceiling, willing it to ebb away. I have a job to do. I don't need any distractions.

I go to see Captain Kohler after breakfast. He has our exams in front of him but I resist taking a peek.

"Captain, I'd like to improve my combat skills."

He seems surprised. "Oh, why is that?" His eyes are piercing, making me ill at ease.

"I don't like having a weakness, sir. I would like to know that if I have to defend myself, I could." He examines me carefully.

"Very well. I like your determination. Who will train you?" He sits back in his chair and tilts his head to one side.

"Sir, Mateo is a mixed martial arts teacher, I'm sure he would be willing to give up an hour a day." Despite wanting to look down, I hold Kohler's steady gaze.

"Yes, that's fine; you may train at 6pm every afternoon in the old school hall."

"Thank you, sir."

"I understand that your father is held in the prison here and that you requested to be posted to this town." His voice is coarse and has a permanent, slightly strained, edge to it.

"Yes, sir." I swallow hard.

He holds my gaze with frightening intensity.

"One more thing, Fortis. Your exam results are very… impressive."

There is something in his voice that puts me even further on edge.

"Thank you, sir."

He wipes his hands on his trousers. "I'd like you to join me in Intelligence."

I allow myself a small smile.

"I can see that's what you wanted."

"Yes, it is. I appreciate the opportunity."

As I leave, I can't shake the notion that there's another reason he wants me working with him.

After seeing Kohler, I help the others with the unloading and distribution of supplies — food and water for the civilians, medicine for the doctor's surgery. The army has one truck to itself, food, water, and medical supplies. We each have six times the supplies we'd just distributed for 30,000 people. Unequal distribution of assets — it's hardly demonstration of the brighter, safer, fairer future the GDO has promised. Not that there was anything wrong with the future we were looking at a year ago, but you can't reason with a tyrant.

I have my first lesson with Mateo that evening; fortunately, language isn't an issue as training is visual. I warm up with sprints and then he starts me on the basics — balance and a few moves. He makes me do press-ups, squats, lunges, dips, and some other moves I can't name, but my muscles tremble from the strain. After an hour, my body is wrecked. This is going to be harder than I thought. Sensing my wavering resolve, Mateo gives me one of his signature wide grins. "It get easy soon, then you fight like championy." He leaps into the air, his lean body flexing, and does a high kick, which I have no doubt would flatten an opponent.

"Me little but fight biggy."

I can't help but laugh. "Thanks Mateo. When I'm finally kicking butt, I'll think of you."

I'm not sure if he understands me but he laughs and smacks me on the back. As I'm leaving the training room I clock the camera that tracks my movement. I swallow down my fear and make my way back to our room.

I am relieved that we have the luxury of hot water again, even though I am still sweating. I turn the shower up in the hope it will help my muscles. The boys are in the dorm waiting for me so we can go and eat together; it's sweet of them really. It feels good to be one of their number, to be part of a team. Like them, I'm dressed in our "off duty" uniform — Prussian blue loose cargo trousers with either a matching t-shirt or cotton shirt.

In the mess hall, the once school dining hall, there are long wooden tables with benches. We collect our food on trays and find a table with enough room for us. The other soldiers sitting on the same table introduce themselves — Greek, France, Naples, and Kilt.

Jono asks what we're all thinking. "What's with the names?"

Greek answers on behalf of the others. "It's where we are all from, it just happened, you know?"

"Yeah, like Drummer's nickname… it just *happened*."

Drummer thumps Jono's arm. "There's a lady present."

"Fortis ain't no lady." Jono winks at me. "So Drummer, well, when he was about thirteen his mum caught him *drumming* away, three times, on the same day."

I can't help but laugh.

"The best part, his first name is Hugh…"

Simon shrugs, "So?"

I look at Drummer's uniform. "Oh no! How could your parents do that to you?" I'm laughing so much my eyes begin to tear up. Simon is staring at Drummer's shirt.

"I don't get it!" Simon is beginning to get frustrated.

"His last name is Cumber… Hugh Cumber."

Simon looks confused and begins muttering "Hugh Cumber" to himself until the two words run together and he finally figures out what we are all laughing at.

"Dude." Kilt seems sympathetic.

Drummer just shakes his head. "My parents were idiots." He looks up and offers the heavens a frown.

A beautiful girl enters and Naples calls to her to join us.

She sits down next to me. "Hi, I'm Goa… Yeah, I know, I tried to convince them India was better but as I'm from Goa and they think it sounds like Goer… Boys…" She rolls her eyes and I give her a sympathetic smile in response.

"Cassia. I'm just waiting for this lot to start the nicknames." I jerk my head towards the boys. "What's your actual name?"

"Shreya."

I repeat her name in my head to make sure I remember it. "It's nice to meet another girl."

"Tell me about it, I've been here for three weeks without another woman to talk to, it's the closest I've ever been to torture."

I already like her; she isn't like Esme and Camilla who seem born to be soldiers.

"So, how come you joined up?" I wonder if I'm being too personal but she seems okay with it.

"My brother Pranav and I were refugees from Naevena; our dad was a diplomat there, once. We've been to military school and so this seemed like the logical next step."

I introduce her to Luca. "We joined together."

"Refugees?" Luca is looking at Shreya in a way I don't like. "I was, a very long time ago now. Cass has been living with my family for a few months."

Shreya looked perplexed. "So what made you join then?"

We look at each other; it wasn't a question we'd prepared an answer for.

Hesitating, I answer, "We share the same beliefs. We want to keep the peace."

Shreya doesn't seem convinced but Luca's smile charms her into distraction. I'm not very hungry after that.

Later, back in our room the boys are discussing their new roles as guards outside the prison walls.

"What are you doing, Cass? You haven't told us?" For some reason Luca is irritating me.

"Intelligence." I climb into bed.

"Get you, smarty pants." Drummer shakes his bum at me; he's like a kid sometimes.

"That where Kohler is?" Jono seems overly interested.

"Yeah."

"Thought as much."

"What do you mean?" Luca sounds agitated.

"He fancies Fortis, gave her the eye straight off. Going to bang the Captain too so you can become a second lieutenant?" Jono is baiting me but I'm used to it now.

"I'm sure you'll do all you can to get in there first."

Simon and Drummer laugh at my retort.

Luca gets into bed whilst the others start talking about Jono and Kohler.

"So, this thing with Kohler…"

I rolled my eyes at Luca. "Luc, seriously? The guy's a creep."

Luca appears pleased. "Doesn't mean I won't make second lieutenant before you though."

I turn over in my bed.

"Uh oh, is that a lover's tiff?" Jono sidles over to our beds.

"Cassia is just upset because she had an unfortunate mental image of you with Kohler," Luca replies. I smile under my duvet, despite myself.

The others go to bed but I can't sleep, despite my body's exhaustion. I keep picturing Luca with Shreya. What is wrong with me? Maybe I'm just jealous that he is making friends with another girl. I enjoy being the only girl in the group; it makes me feel special. No, that's ridiculous; I have to learn to stop being such a brat about things, and share.

The next morning, I make my way to the old radio station building where Intelligence is based. My first day is just learning how everything works. One wall is filled with small screens showing the feeds from the security cameras around the town. Information from other regiments is constantly being fed in, and we have to review it all in case there's anything important. There are a few families and people under surveillance in the town, and we have to keep track of their movements. Then there's SINN — the Secure Internal

Network Nucleus. It was set up by the GDO a few years ago and works like a server; every single intelligence system in the GDO network is linked to SINN. It's almost like an Internet resource; you can find out anything you want to know just by using the search function. Jaidee, a technician from Thailand, shows me SINN.

"So, where is the main server then?"

"In old Spain." We use the prefix 'old' before countries a lot now.

"Is that the main GDO headquarters then? I thought it was in old Switzerland, I mean, Naevena?" Jaidee shakes his head.

"That's where the headquarters were before Cooper Anderson took over…"

"And the war started. Oh, I didn't realise." I rub my neck in concentration. "So, we're linked to the main server that's in old… I mean, in Utonia?"

"Think of it like the Internet, and the server in Utonia is the Internet's brain."

I nod in understanding. "So, for instance, if we had a difficult situation we could instantly connect to Utonia, where the main GDO base is, and they could help us?"

"Exactly. It enables direct communication with each zone in each country and we receive direct orders from head office in Utonia."

I smile; my lesson is proving incredibly valuable. "Wow, that's incredible."

"Yeah, so a few weeks ago we heard about a riot in Degeland (the capital of Naevena) and the Utonian GDO helped them by turning the satellites to watch the uprising. They then coordinated the troops from there. Remarkable use of technology." Jaidee seems genuinely impressed. It unsettles me to think there are people who actually support the GDO.

"It really is." My mind is flicking through scenarios where SINN could be of use.

I am introduced to the other people on my team: Harold, Claude, Elliot, and Sven.

We are all scheduled to work nights and I manage to get Captain Kohler to coincide my shifts with my roommates and Mateo, so I can keep up with my training. Friday afternoon we have more gun training and the boys work out whilst I'm with Mateo. We're already starting to settle into a routine.

That evening our first night shift starts. We will work nights from Friday through to Monday morning, then a day off to recover, and back to work on Wednesday. By making sure my shifts are the same as the boys, I'm on the same rota as Harold, who I have already pegged as lazy. It's a lucky break.

It's sort of spooky in the old radio station at night. Lights blink from the equipment and it's the same oppressive quiet that every town and city suffers from. Curfew feels like a curse has fallen over the town, forcing it into silence.

By 11pm, Harold is yawning and at midnight, he's fast asleep and snoring. I may not have been able to deactivate building security like Yve but I have always been a closet computer nerd. I'd taken a course at school on programming and I can read and create code. A friend of mine, Clive, is a computer genius. Instead of listening to our boring teacher in our computer lessons, Clive would teach me how to hack into things like the school administration files without having our IP address traced, how to order one hundred pizzas from the school's budget for lunch, and how to access the new games for his Elite 5 games console pre-release. All the while, Mr Rogers taught a class who were mostly self-taught in code, how to do it anyway.

I figure that if everything is connected, and that the main server is in Utonia, then I can access confidential information from the main database. SINN is the GDO's Achilles heel. If I were able to get information without being detected, I'd find a way to bring down their network. Without the ability to coordinate their different territories from Utonia, the GDO would be significantly weakened; with SINN down it would be the perfect time to disable them further. I'm just not sure what that part of the plan will be yet.

I start by getting to know SINN, looking for weaknesses so that I can create a "back door" for future entry. Then even if the system is upgraded I would have my way in. At 4am, I stop. I'm too tired to concentrate any more and I can't risk a mistake. I kick Harold's chair to wake him up.

"Mind if I shut my eyes for a bit? I'm really sleepy."

"What time is it?" Harold can't focus.

"4am."

He looks surprised. "You let me sleep 'til four? Thanks, Fortis! Claude would only let me have two thirty-minute naps."

I smile at him. "Tell you what. I'll let you sleep until I can't hack it and then I'll wake you and you can take over. Deal?"

Harold looks thrilled. "Yeah, definitely. I'm glad you're on my rota."

"Thanks Harold, me too."

At 5:45am, Harold wakes me up with a cup of tea; the day shift comes in at 6am.

I arrive back in the dorm before the boys and I get straight into bed. I barely hear them get in ten minutes later.

Adjusting to night shifts isn't easy and on Sunday, I'm restless.

"Can't sleep either?" Luca props himself up on his elbow and talks to me in a whisper.

I shake my head. "Going to see if I can get a lift to Amphora to see my mum. We're allowed to do that on Sundays, visit our families?" I ask and rub my aching eyes.

"Yeah, you know what? I want to see mine too. I'll come with you," Luca replies.

I am excited by the prospect of having Luca to myself again. "You don't have to, you need the sleep."

"I want to, I miss them. Besides, it'll give us a chance to talk without that lot listening in."

Drummer snores as if on cue.

There's a truck going to Amphora to collect some supplies, and so long as we're back by 2pm we're allowed to jump in the back. Luca and I chat for a bit but the gentle rocking of the vehicle and the warm day sends us to sleep. I wake up in Amphora with my head resting on Luca's shoulder. I am so happy and comfortable there that I don't want to move, but I see the driver getting out of the truck and so I shake Luca gently awake. Luca opens his eyes and smiles sweetly at me. My heart flutters. What is up with me? We say goodbye and I make my way to the hospital. I have to wait around for visiting hours but it's nice just to walk around and relax a little.

Mum is looking much better; she's been eating properly and is sitting up without too much trouble. I am so relieved I nearly cry. She is hoping to be released from hospital in a few weeks.

"What do you mean, Mum?"

"Well, they think I'm in remission, but they are keeping me in for observation because it's such a quick turnaround and they want to be cautious."

I nearly crush her still-fragile body with my hug. "If I can get you housed in Camburg, will you be happy to go there? There's a doctor's surgery there that could do with a good nurse."

"How would you manage that?"

I give her a knowing smile. "Oh, my captain should be able to swing it."

"Well, if it isn't too much trouble, I would love to be near you and your father."

I kiss her cheek. With Mum in Camburg, I can reunite my parents. If I know they're together, safe and happy, then I'll have the strength to keep going with my plan.

My step is lighter as I leave the hospital; Luca is standing waiting for me and grins when he notices my light mood.

It's then that I run into Jake. I throw myself at him, giving him a big hug, but his body seizes up at my touch.

"Jake, it's so good to see you!"

He pushes me away and looks down at my uniform in disgust. "So, this is where you've been? I thought you and Luca were at a work camp for doing something stupid. Guess you are more stupid than I originally thought."

I can understand his anger; it looks like I've joined forces with the people who killed his parents, destroyed his life.

"No, Jake, you don't understand." I look around to check no one's listening and lower my voice. "Luca and I are trying to find a way to help."

Jake grabs my arm, hard. "Is that your excuse? You're just a murderer like the rest of them."

I can't speak. Why doesn't he understand?

"Jake, let her go." Luca is behind Jake, looking tall and powerful in comparison. Jake turns to look at Luca and spits at his feet.

"Jake, we're finding a way to make things better, for everyone."

Jake's eyes blaze. "By joining the enemy? That's your big plan? You're both idiots, you're just like them. You're just like all of them — Crones. I want nothing to do with either of you."

He storms off and I look up at Luca.

"I'm sorry, Cassia, I know that..."

I cut Luca off. "He's a friend Luc, it's not like that, but... I have just hurt my oldest friend. Do you think we can make him understand?"

Luca puts his arm around me. "I think he's too angry at the moment to see reason. I don't blame him; I am too, but he's been through more than us."

I lean into his body. "Yeah, he has, I just hope he calms down before he does something stupid."

We go back to our pick-up point in silence. Seeing Jake is making me doubt our plan; what if we have joined our enemy and we don't make things better for the people we love? What does that make Luca and me? Traitors?

I stare out of the back of the truck as we drive back to Camburg. Luca and I are alone. His hand brushes against mine, and then links our fingers. We sit that way, in silence, the whole way back. We're back in our dorm by 3pm, the others still sound asleep. As I'm about to get into bed Luca comes up behind me and wraps his arms around my waist.

"I'm sorry, Cass."

My heart is racing and my cheeks flush. I tell myself he's just being a good friend but I keep his arms around me all the same. I don't know how long we stand like that.

"It's not all bad. Mum's getting better." I turn to face him, my cheeks no longer red.

"That's incredible." His hand touches my arm.

"How are your family?"

"They're doing well, keeping in good spirits as always."

"I miss them."

"Me too."

We stand there looking at each other and for a moment, I think, I think that maybe Luca will kiss me. I feel a mixture of panic and excitement. Instead, he kisses the top of my head and his hand brushes against my arm as he gets into his bed. "Sleep well."

WEEK SEVEN

I wake up late and have to rush to shower and make it down to the Intelligence building; I am feeling sick with lack of sleep, and need coffee. Fortunately, Harold is way ahead of me — when I get to my desk there's a fresh cup waiting.

"Thanks, Harold."

He looks pleased with himself; I'm not sure he usually does favours.

"Nights are rough and the first time is the worst. Besides, if you're going to stay alert whilst I'm sleeping you're going to need that."

I'm right. He isn't doing me a favour really; he's just making sure he gets his sleep. I hold back my mental groan and smile at him as sweetly as I can. At least he'll be asleep most of the time and I won't have to deal with him.

Harold immediately settles down to sleep on the small sofa at the back of the room. When his snores are regular and rhythmic, I go to the door and stand out of view of the camera and then place a sticky note over the lens that points into the office — not particularly clever or subtle, but I don't have time to locate where the feed leads to and set it on a loop. I go back to work. I enter SINN and find my way to the Utonia database. I don't want the obvious files; I'm looking for anything hidden.

After two hours of hacking, another cup of coffee, and numerous curses that I'm not a better hacker, I manage to bypass the final firewall. There is only one folder, which doesn't even have a file name. I open it and inside are hundreds of documents and files. I don't have enough time to open them all so I use a secure file transferring system to put them in an online drop box. The drop box system was set up by hackers. It's almost impossible to detect the file has been copied from an outside source, and even if they do notice, it's impossible to track where the copy went. Even with the Internet no longer accessible by citizens (there aren't any public phone or broadband companies anymore), there is always a way in the hacker world. The download is going to take forty-five minutes. I look at Harold, worried he'll wake up.

Thirty minutes, Harold is still asleep. Twenty minutes, no change. Ten minutes, and I can tell he's stirring. I switch my monitor off and concentrate on the security footage.

I hear his body shift position. "Fortis, what's the time?"

"Just after four."

"You let me sleep longer, nice one."

"I can take over now." I turn to him and smile sweetly. "Why don't you make yourself a coffee so you're alert? I can wait five more minutes."

"Yeah, I could do with a piss as well." Lovely.

When he's gone I look at the download: three minutes thirty-five seconds remaining. I begin to tap my foot impatiently. The toilet door shuts and I hear Harold filling up the kettle in the kitchen. Two minutes.

One minute.

Thirty seconds.

Harold is coming in.

"Hey, Harold — can you grab me a glass of water?"

His tone is reluctant. "Yeah, fine."

Three seconds.

Harold enters. The download is complete and I've had time to shut everything down. I've set the system to automatically wipe my digital footprints. I'm better at this than I thought; maybe espionage has been my calling all along. I get up to go to the toilet and as I pass I remember the sticky note. I flick it off when Harold's back is turned.

Later that morning I manage to sleep but I'm woken up by Luca at 12pm. I put my pillow over my head.

"Cass, come on, you won't sleep tonight otherwise."

"Sleep, need sleep."

He pulls my covers off me and so I kick him. He grabs my leg and pulls me so that my head isn't under my pillow. And then he steals my pillow.

"Luc, I swear I am going to… to…" I pinch him. He picks me up and throws me over his shoulder. "LUC!" The rest of the boys are now awake and grumbling at us. A few pillows are thrown our way.

Luca heads to the bathroom, "No, Luc, don't you dare." He turns the shower on and moves the dial to cold. "Luc, I am warning you."

"Morning, Cass." He dumps me under the freezing water and I let out a scream. I grab him and pull him in with me, and he lets out a deep bellow.

"Asshole."

He starts laughing and strolls out of the shower. His white t-shirt clings to his muscular body — I am unexpectedly grateful to be in a cold shower.

"Let's go for a run, it'll sort you out."

I glower at him but I need to expend some energy; the image of Luca's wet torso will haunt me all day otherwise.

Luca is outside stretching, waiting for me. We start with a slow jog through the town and the guards let us through the main gate once we've been ID'd.

"Where we going?"

Luca points to the dense expanse of trees on our left, which eventually open out onto a lake.

We keep our pace slow, allowing our bodies to get used to the rhythm and for our muscles to wake up. Once we're in the woods Luca starts doing sprints — sprint then jog, sprint then jog. I join in, enjoying the strain on my body. By the time we reach the lake I'm shattered. Luca heads straight for the water and I follow happily. The water is cool and clear; I lie back and wait for my breathing to settle.

When I've cooled down I look around.

"So, I've been working on something…"

Luca looks at me; he knows what I mean. "What have you found?"

"The GDO has a network called SINN, all their servers are connected, even their ones in Utonia."

Luca furrows his brow. "That's pretty careless."

"Not if you're the supremo power. I suppose you get arrogant and don't think anyone can penetrate your security. Besides, with no cellular or Internet access for the general public, who's to hack them?"

Luca looks at me — alright, I would hack them, but that's not my point.

"Don't you find it strange they let us into the army, barely any questions asked?"

I haven't told him about my conversation with Kohler. I focus on the sky. The clouds above swirl together in a dance; it's hypnotising, beautiful, and almost makes me forget that I'm a prisoner in my own country.

"To them, we're just two kids, hardly a threat."

Luca's eyes are looking straight into mine and I force myself to concentrate.

"Anyway, I found my way into Utonia's secret database and transferred some files to a secure drop box."

Luca smiles at me with admiration. "Well done, that's incredible. Will they notice?"

"Shouldn't do. I was careful." My tone is nonchalant.

"What next?"

"I'll make copies of the file, keep them in separate secure locations. One or two will have to be on physical hard drives and then, I plant a virus."

Luca swims closer to me. "You're a genius, you know that?"

I feel embarrassed; I'm not a genius, I'm just lucky. For the time being at least.

"I can't think what we'd do with SINN down. If only we could let people know it was happening so they could, I don't know, take control of their own towns… I'm no good at this military planning."

Luca treads water as he thinks. "Well, you figure out how to get word out, and I'll work on a plan to get the political prisoners out."

"You think it's enough of a diversion to save Dad?" Luca's grin makes my stomach flutter.

"Yeah, I think it is."

Luca begins swimming away from me.

"We'll need help, Luc."

"You know the boys will, they're not here out of patriotism, or whatever it is you're supposed to feel towards the GDO." He dives under water and there are only ripples on the surface to indicate where he has been. I watch as the water flows outwards from that single point.

Can we really ask them to risk everything for us? Will they actually be willing to help and not turn us in? My instincts say yes, but it's still a huge gamble.

Luca's hand grabs my ankle and pulls me down under the water; I have just enough time to take a breath. My eyes are open and I can see his grin. He pulls my body to him and then lifts me out of the water. I drink in the fresh air.

"You know, sometimes it's okay to let your hair down."

I laugh at Luca. "When have you ever let your hair down?"

He seems genuinely offended. "I have fun."

"Sure, but not lately."

He swims towards me and, grasping my sides, throws me up into the air so that I come down with an almighty splash. "See, I'm having fun right now."

"I'm not!"

He swims towards me and I back away. "No, no more."

I keep swimming but he's faster, and catches up until his body is touching mine. "No more, I promise."

He's so close to me, I can feel his warm breath against my neck. His lips brush along my cheek and then we are face to face. My body is trembling with anticipation. He leans in so close that I can almost feel the kiss before it happens, and then there's a crack of gunfire from the south. We both pull away and look towards the sound.

"Maybe we should get back, I don't want us caught in the middle of something when we're unarmed."

We swim to the shore and carefully pick our way through the trees, keeping an eye out for anyone else. If we encounter any anti-GDO groups, we'll be in trouble; all our clothes are military issue. Our running kit is a charcoal t-shirt and tracksuit bottoms with GDO ARMY in white on the back, and all our clothes have our names embroidered on the front left. We are hardly inconspicuous.

When we are through the trees we can see that we're alone and so begin the jog back to base to try and dry off. We don't say anything on our run back, nothing about the kiss that almost was. I am feeling really confused. Does Luca actually like me, or is he just playing games?

Near camp Luca stops and grabs hold of my arm. I freeze and scan our surroundings; there's movement to our left, so we both drop low and wait.

Luca indicates for me to stay but I glower at him and indicate that we flank the area we think the person is hiding in. As I creep closer to our target it finally hits me; I'm unarmed, with no bulletproof vest and no helmet, heading towards someone who may have been rattling off gunfire not too long ago.

Our plan doesn't seem so brilliant anymore. As we stalk through the woods in silence my heartbeat slows. We haven't heard any noises in a while. Luca signals to hold and we crouch down lower simultaneously, scanning the trees. Nothing, not even the sound of birds. Not a good sign.

I spot a small movement and signal to Luca. We roll our feet as we walk to minimise the crackle of twigs and leaves. Lying camouflaged is a man with his rifle tucked under his arm; he's sweating heavily.

Luca nods to me and I lunge for the man, drawing his attention. He goes for his rifle but Luca is on him and he's quickly subdued with Luca's knee in his back.

"Why are you here?" Luca whispers into the man's ear. His tone is threatening; a soldier's tone.

"I — I got split from the rest of my group."

Luca looks down at the man and I can see he doesn't know what to do. I look around and no one seems to have noticed us. I nod to Luca.

"Listen to me. We're going to let you go but I'm keeping the rifle, do you understand?" The man bobs his head emphatically.

"Leave quietly, slowly. Draw attention to us and I shoot you in the back. Got it?" Even I believed Luca so I was 100% sure the man did too.

We watch him go and Luca buries the rifle — we can't go back in with a new weapon. I'm already worried we've drawn attention to ourselves for being gone so long.

I start to feel sick the closer we get to the gates, partly because of the adrenalin draining and also from the realisation of who we are. We are soldiers for our enemy, and with that comes the duty to act out their orders, whatever they may be. We were lucky that this time we were alone.

Needing a distraction, I head to Mateo's flat and as I knock on the door I can hear a baby crying. A slight woman in her thirties opens the door; she has a warm, friendly face.

"Hi, I'm Cassia, I thought I'd come and introduce myself."

"I'm Milena." A small boy of two runs up and grabs his mother's leg. "This is Tomas, and over there is Valentina." She signals for me to come in.

"Hi, Mateo."

"Hi, Cassia, is nice to see you." He bounces Valentina in his arms.

"We were going to take the children to the park, would you like to join us?" Milena begins stuffing nappies and bottles of water and other baby bits into a bag. Simon told me that Milena used to work as a hotel receptionist, which explains why her English is much better than Mateo's.

"There's a park?" I look out of the window at the bleak town, bewildered it has something so fun.

"A small one, it has a slide and two swings. Better than nothing."

"I'd love to." I pick up the bag for Milena.

Tomas holds my hand all the way to the park and insists I'm the one to push him on the swing.

"Do you miss your home?" I ask Milena — her eyes are sad.

"Every day. But the place I knew, it's not there now. Most of the cities were destroyed."

I don't understand; the GDO didn't go that far afield during the season of riots. "Destroyed?"

"Yes, destroyed, during the chaos, with the riots, our government used force to regain control. They destroyed most of the cities, that's when we fled here. It was peaceful here."

Something is starting to click in my brain.

"So, the news reports we received, they were false? How did they manage that, when there were still free nations?"

Milena shrugs. "When you have enough money and power you can buy your own story. The government didn't want people to know what they had done. They didn't want the world to see that they had torn apart their own country. Foreign press wasn't allowed in; our press was silenced."

I have been so naïve. I thought that the impact around the globe was the same as here but some of it must have been worse, much worse. It wasn't just us who suffered. Yes, we were under the GDO's control, but we weren't the only people whose lives have been ripped apart.

"How many people died?"

"They think over a million."

My stomach drops. "A million? How can that be?"

"Most of San Paolo was destroyed and the hunger, the hunger killed a lot of people."

I sit down on the swing next to Tomas. I remember it; the food shortages in cities when the riots started and we were getting information through the news. One of the biggest problem was that food couldn't get into the cities — people were trapped and starving. They were rioting for freedom but they signed their own death sentence.

"Over a million people in one nation. How many have been murdered in total since the riots over here because of the GDO?"

It isn't a question that Milena can answer. "We just have to protect those we love now, no matter what; we have to do what we can to keep them safe."

Valentina is in her arms and her little hand is reaching up to touch her mother's cheek. I look across at Mateo who is looking thoughtful.

"My family need safe."

I understand what he means; he is doing his best for them. "You do what you need." I look at Mateo, really look, and he nods. "I know what you here for. I know. You do it but I must keep family okay."

"I know Mateo, thank you; I'm going to do everything I can so that your children can grow up in a better world." Valentina grabs my finger with her fist and holds on tight. "Absolutely everything I can."

I am feeling in a pensive mood when I make my way to supper in the mess. The boys are all together and Luca and Shreya are sitting at one end, deep in conversation with Naples. I sit down at the opposite end next to Simon.

"Where've you been?"

"With Mateo and his family." I take a bite of my bread; it tastes slightly sour in my mouth,

"His kids are cute aren't they?" Simon is relaxed and smiling.

"Yeah, really cute." My soup tastes bitter. I push it to one side and take a bite of my apple instead.

"Something the matter?"

I look into Simon's face; he's lost more than me, most people have. I'm lucky my family is still alive, and I am privileged to be eating a meal and to be around friends. "No, just, rough day."

Simon places his hand over mine. "Yeah, I know."

I pull my hand away. "Sorry, I'm crappy company today. I think I'm just going to head upstairs."

He nods and I leave. I can feel Luca's eyes following me.

I sit on the end of my bed and think about all those lives that had been destroyed by the GDO. How had the GDO managed to succeed? It doesn't seem possible when you really think about it. Not even the US intervened, but at the time they had their own problems and I guess they just let the disaster over here play out.

I've only been with the army a short time but I've already seen that they garner a lot of loyalty and I can't quite comprehend it — yes, we have food, shelter for our families, and decent pay, but that doesn't outweigh the destruction they've caused. Are so many people without a conscience? Or do many just feel that there really is no other option and it's the only way to protect their families? If that's true, then the GDO has a larger problem than two teenage spies.

I am asleep by the time the others come into our dorm. Luca tries to wake me but I ignore him and drift back to sleep.

Wednesday is my day off but I can't fit in a visit to my mum, so instead Mateo agrees to train me. I push myself harder than I have before. My muscles shake and burn but I keep on pushing. I won't be a victim. I refuse to be a victim just because I live in a time of occupation. At the end of the session I manage to floor Mateo. He pats me on the back; I am improving already. Unsure what to do with the rest of my time off I spend my afternoon walking around the town, assessing the set-up. Most of the shops are shut, blank spaces in an oppressively empty high street. They have built a fence around the entire town, nothing particularly sturdy, and there are guards at certain points to allow entry in and out, and to keep watch. I make my way to the prison, which has its own security in place; there's a double fence and a wall. The guards are in raised towers, all armed. All the old inmates were moved to another facility. This building only houses the political prisoners because it's the closet one to Amphora. At least I won't have to worry about releasing dangerous criminals back out into the world.

The prison is close to one of the gates out of the town — that will be our exit point.

Luca corners me in the dining hall. "What's up with you? Haven't seen you all day."

I shrug. "Been training with Mateo and had some things to do."

"Cass, what's up? Is this about the other day?"

I feign disinterest. "What do you mean?" I sit down with the others.

"Come on, don't be like this."

I look up at him. "Like what?"

He lets out a frustrated sigh and focuses on his food.

Shreya sits down with us, along with Greek and Naples; I smile at them as they sit down.

Shreya leans forward. "Hey, Luca, how've you been?"

Luca smiles back at her. "Yeah, good, the boys and I have been working out this afternoon."

"I can see that."

I start choking on my mouthful of potato; Drummer smacks me hard on the back until I recover.

"Cheers, Drum."

"No problem, partner." Drummer looks over at Shreya and Luca. "What's up with those two?" His voice is a low whisper.

"Don't know. Think there's something there?"

Drummer looks at me. "You know he's totally into you, right?"

"Don't be stupid." Despite myself I find I'm very interested in Drummer's point of view.

"Look, if you act all stubborn he's just going to end up with Goa and then you'll be moody all the time, and I don't want that. It's bad enough when you're running on four hours' sleep, being slighted for another woman..." He lets out a whistle.

I hold my fork up and point it at him. "Just… drop it okay, there's nothing going on, and he can be with her if he wants to."

"Women."

I steal his pudding cup as punishment and leave the dining hall. The place is starting to stifle me.

The next day Kohler calls me into his office to ask me why I'd been standing outside the prison the day before. I explain that I miss my father and, yes, I'm aware there aren't any visiting privileges and no, I wasn't spying. I left feeling even more certain that I've made a terrible mistake joining the GDO.

The rest of the week goes on as normal, except I have to work Sunday. It's the hardest day of the week because every minute I'm there with the army, I could be in Amphora with my mum.

WEEK EIGHT

Monday is my last normal work day. I'll start nights again on Tuesday, which means I'll be able to make copies of the files I've stolen. I just need a hard drive. There are a few in the office but they're being used, so I need to locate one that won't be missed.

There's only an hour left of my shift and I'm feeling restless. I need to get away from computer screens and security feeds. As I'm stretching out my aching legs one of the monitors draws my attention; I squint at the small figures and send the feed from the camera to my computer so I can see it full screen. A woman is walking down the street carrying a bundle in her arms. Two soldiers are pointing their guns at her and they seem to be yelling, but she's ignoring them.

"Captain? We have a situation." Kohler leans over my shoulder and his hot sticky breath smells like bitter day-old garlic.

"Another terrorist, I better get down there." He slicks back his hair as he makes to leave.

"Sir, I don't think that's the situation, she's not carrying a bomb."

Kohler smirks at me. "Still a naïve little private aren't you?"

I bite my tongue. "I'm coming with you." I stand up to attention.

"Very well." He radios in the threat and instructs the soldiers to hold fire until he has assessed the situation first hand.

By the time we arrive there are five soldiers surrounding the woman. She is shaking but she's still not responding to the soldier's commands to put down the package; instead she just clings tighter to it.

Kohler calls for nearby soldiers to clear the area then he steps forward towards the woman. "Just put the package on the floor and walk away."

Her eyes look into his beseechingly. I am standing right behind Kohler, and that's when I understand what she's holding. Her hand moves and the soldiers start yelling at her all at once. I can see where things are going — one soldier is shaking, his hand on the trigger. Kohler pulls out his gun and is aiming at her head. "Put down the package or I shoot you, on the count of three. One."

An innocent woman is about to die. I can't stand by and do nothing.

"Two."

I push my way past Kohler and the soldiers and stand in front of the woman. Kohler glares at me.

"Sir, she's not a threat."

My insolence enrages him but he steadies himself. "You are out of line, Fortis."

I ignore him and turn to the woman, speaking to her in a low voice. "It's okay, I understand. I'm so sorry, I'm so very sorry. I just need to show them, so they won't hurt you."

She begins sobbing; very slowly I bring my hand forward and pull back the blanket that covers what she's holding. It falls away and underneath is her baby. He's no longer breathing. I turn to Kohler who waves the soldiers away and walks back to the office. The woman falls to her knees and I hold her until her tears stop and her body slumps, exhausted. I help her back to her small flat, which she shares with two men and three women.

When I leave her home I stand in the empty street. They would have killed her; they couldn't see who people were anymore — everybody is a potential threat. Is their humanity really that far gone? War had shown me dead bodies before but a baby, a baby is different. It's far more haunting. The GDO didn't kill him but they would have killed his mother. They are frightened of anything they can't control; they are weak after all.

Eventually I begin moving. I don't go back into the Intelligence lab, but instead I go to the dorm, get changed into a tracksuit, and begin to run. I run harder and faster than I have before, and soon find myself at the lake. I stand until the tears come, burning hot. I fall to my knees and cover my face in my hands as I scream out my frustration. No more innocent lives. No more.

When I have regained my composure I run back, shower and change into my blues, and head off for supper. I pick up a tray and collect my pasta and a fruit salad. As I reach the table where the others are, Kohler approaches me.

"My office. Now." There is no mistaking how angry he is that I've shown him up. All eyes follow me and Kohler out of the room.

In his office Kohler marches across the room and stands behind his desk, his position of power. He is breathing heavily. "How *dare* you disobey my order?"

"Sir…"

He holds up his hand. "Not only did you go against the command of a superior, you *dared* to do it in front of a civilian and other soldiers. Do you have any idea how this makes our regiment look, how it makes *me* look?!"

"Sir." He glares at me but I carry on. "Our orders are to maintain the peace. If that woman had been shot, we could have had riots on our hands. You put me in Intelligence for a reason, I assessed the situation, I knew she wasn't a threat."

Kohler's face is practically purple. "You do NOT speak back to me, you do not tell me that you think you are right and I am wrong. If I tell you to shoot a kitten, you shoot the bloody kitten. If I tell you to kiss your mother's murderer, you damn well kiss them. I am your captain. You do exactly as I say." He steps forward and thrusts his face right up against mine. "And if I see even one keystroke, one shoe lace, one hair out of place, I will report you. You've already been displaying suspicious behaviour, Fortis. Just one more misstep and you're mine. You are on nights for five days' straight and you will spend the rest of today cleaning all the toilets in the barracks."

I look at him directly in the eye. I won't be intimidated and I want him to know that. "Yes, sir."

Cleaning the toilets is never as bad as it sounds, as someone is always being given it as a punishment. I am on my knees cleaning what must be my tenth toilet when there's a knock on the cubicle door. It swings open and Luca is staring down at me.

"Having fun?"

I smile. "The most fun ever." I wave the toilet brush at him as if it were a magic wand.

"Can I give you a hand?"

"No, thanks. You'll just get in trouble and he'll find more toilets for me to clean."

"Okay. So, this is about the situation earlier?"

I push myself off the floor. "You heard?"

"Sort of, you know what rumours are like; I thought it was better coming from the source."

I peek around the cubicle into the bathroom; no one else is around. Fortunately, they haven't installed a camera in the toilets — yet.

"They thought a woman was a terrorist, but she was just holding her baby bundled up in his blanket. He was dead Luca, she was in shock." I have been trying to suppress the image but talking about it just brings it straight back.

"That's awful…" Luca shakes his head. "So, why is Kohler mad at you?"

I pull at my rubber gloves. "I showed him up by stopping him and the other soldiers shooting her."

Luca mouths, "Wow."

"Yeah, he's pretty annoyed."

"It'll blow over." He squeezes my shoulder.

"Yeah, five night shifts should do it."

"Ouch." He wrinkles his nose and I respond with a small smile.

"Actually, he's giving me what I want... I can probably turn things around quicker this way."

Luca brushes my hair from my face. "Now that's one way to find a silver lining." He smiles at me, kisses me on the cheek, and then leaves. Turns out that cleaning toilets really isn't so bad after all.

Kohler makes me work Tuesday day as well. It's hot outside and sitting in a room with one small window and a lot of overheating machinery is unbearable. Sven and Jaidee go to the dining hall to see if there's any ice or even ice cream to cool us off. I'm left alone with Kohler.

"You know, my office has a fan in it. If you behave I could bring it in here."

I smile at him despite his offer sounding more like a threat. "Thank you, sir, but I'm sure we'll manage." I don't want to owe him anything. I can feel a bead of sweat making its way down between my cleavage. We'll survive, but we'll probably be shrivelled and dehydrated by the end of the day.

At six, Claude and Jaidee leave. Sven is on the late afternoon shift with me. Kohler marches in.

"Fortis, get your dinner now and then straight back here." If movement didn't make me sweat, I would punch his smugly face.

The more time I spend with Kohler, the more I dislike him. He does that thing that creepy men do when they talk to girls — he hitches his belt, like he's thinking of something inappropriate about you. What makes it worse is that I know he's watching my every move and possibly reporting to someone higher up; his gaze is like a prison sentence.

The boys aren't in the dining room when I arrive, but I can see Shreya. I sit down with her. She seems welcoming, but I can feel a hint of jealousy coming from her.

I push aside my feelings; I don't need any more anger in my life. "Whereabouts are you based?"

"Inside the prison."

I try not to reveal my personal interest in her work place. I glance around; the room was noisy, the cameras far away. It's safe for me to pry a little.

"Must be baking in there."

"It's like a giant sweat box. We've been handing out water to the inmates all day." She relaxes a little. "Where are you?"

"Intelligence, a small sweat box."

"So you're clever, that's cool." She doesn't seem happy about it.

"What's the prison like? They all in tiny cells and stuff?" I chew on my overcooked chicken casually to try and keep myself from appearing too eager.

"They've crammed everyone in with bunk beds — four to a room."

"I always thought prison cells were two to a room."

Shreya shrugs.

"Are the inmates violent?" I widen my eyes, pretending I am searching for juicy gossip.

Shreya looks sad. "A lot are depressed, drag their feet around. Most of them are nice, you know. They're not proper criminals, just prisoners of war. Sometimes you'll get someone lose their temper, but I don't blame them."

"Sounds awful — must be hard."

She shrugs again but I can tell she doesn't like it in there.

"What's Intelligence like? Do you get juicy intel?"

I laugh; the actual job is hardly juicy. "No, it's just monitoring. Staring at a computer, really, nothing exciting."

I hear the boys enter before I see them; Drummer and Jono are never stealthy in their approach to a meal.

Drummer sits down next to me and immediately steals one of my potatoes. "Gotta watch your weight, Fortis."

I take the ice from my water and put it down the back of his shirt. He shudders. "Oh, Fortis, stop being such a tease."

I can't help but laugh. You can't win against Drummer.

Luca sits next to Shreya. I refuse to let myself feel jealous; I can overcome it. I'm a soldier now. My teenage hormones just need to back off.

"It's weirdly hot today, it's like summer's come early." Simon wipes the back of his neck with a paper towel. He is pale skinned and looks like he's really suffering, his face red, his hair slick to his head.

"It is June." Jono informs him.

"Already? I don't seem to know what day of the week it is." Simon gulps down his water.

"Dude, I think you might have heat exhaustion." Drummer pats Simon's back and then regrets it — his shirt is soaked.

"Just stand in a cold shower for ages and drink a glass of milk. You'll be fine." I smile at him and he nods; he's feeling too rubbish to speak.

"MILK?!" All the boys ask at once, incredulous.

"If you can stand it, it works sort of like a sports drink."

"Fortis, stop talking voodoo." Jono shakes his head at me.

I get up to leave; Luca looks up at me. "Leaving already? Aren't you going to stay and make more wild claims?"

I sigh. "Captain wants me back to complete my entire day of torture. The office is turning into a steam room." Luca smiles and out of the corner of my eye I see Shreya watching us. I walk away trying to convince myself to be the bigger person and not be so competitive.

Outside the heat hits me. The humidity is thick and my skin quickly becomes slick with sweat. The temperature is beginning to mess with me; at least, that's what I'm blaming it on. Who am I kidding? I'm jealous of Shreya; I want to be with Luca. But, what can I do about it? I'm not going to throw myself at him. Freeing my dad from the GDO is a challenge, but liking someone is much harder work and feels a lot riskier. Irritated by the heat and my inability to focus on more important things, I sit down at my computer and wipe the stinging sweat from my eyes so I can see the screen in front of me.

Harold shows up late for work and Kohler is nowhere to be seen. I am worried he won't sleep because of the clinging heat but nothing seems to prevent Harold from enjoying his favourite activity.

At 9pm I hear someone enter the building. I run back to my desk. I've been investigating where the feed for the surveillance camera in our office leads, as I need to start running it on a loop or disable it if I'm going to do any more spy work. Luca walks in.

"What are you doing here? You're going to get into trouble." I flick my eyes to the camera next to him but I can't hide my smile.

"Simon took a turn for the worse so Jono and Drummer raided the kitchen for some ice lollies to cool him off. They got a little carried away; I thought you might like some of their stash." He holds out two lollies.

"You're a life saver. Can't believe it's nearly dark but it's not any cooler." I take a lolly.

"It's the humidity." Luca doesn't look uncomfortable like the rest of us though.

"Simon okay?"

"He'll live. He tried a glass of milk."

"And?"

"Made him gag."

"Oh…"

"But, that's because he hates it. He said he did start to feel better later, and we've been giving him water too. Nice voodoo trick."

I rip open my lolly and relish the cold sweet ice. "You shouldn't stick around, I don't want you getting caught."

Luca smiles mischievously at me. "I'll be fine. Besides, I can hide in that cupboard if anyone comes." He turns and looks at the door behind him.

"The server room? It's the hottest place on earth. One day they're going to overheat and the whole surveillance system here will go down." I roll my eyes at the incompetence of the set-up in Camburg.

"I was born to be warm."

I start laughing but it has given me an idea. "Wow, Luc."

He sits down next to me. "Show me what you've been doing."

I look around, Harold is asleep and I can't hear any movement downstairs.

"Okay, but I really need to find the camera's feed first."

We go out into the hall and I go back to
Kohler's door where I'd been trying to unpick the
lock before. After fiddling with the two paperclips
for a couple of seconds, the door clicks open.

"Careful, he'll have some kind of system set-
up in here too."

"Yes, Mr Obvious."

I go to Kohler's desk and insert the USB
drive with the password hacker Clive gave me
when we were at school, the only thing I brought
with me when I became a Crone. Once I'm logged
on I open up the feeds to the cameras and find the
office ones. I loop it back two hours, and loop
Kohler's own feedback an hour, whilst Luca stands
watch at the door.

"You make it look easy," he says, as we go
back into the main office.

"Only because of Clive."

I open up the online drop box and show
Luca how to access it if he ever needs to. We open
up the file.

"I don't even know where to start with this
stuff." I wipe the sweat from my face with both
hands.

Luca shakes his head. "Neither do I."

I am scrolling through files, trying to decide
which one to open first, when I hear a noise from

downstairs. In a flash Luca is in the server room; it's a tight squeeze but at least he's hidden.

Kohler struts in, looks at Harold and shakes his head. "Looks like you're on your own up here, Fortis."

"Looks like it." I keep my eyes fixed on Kohler; I don't want to look in the direction of Luca's hiding place.

"Anything to report?" He steps closer.

"No, sir, all quiet tonight." I turn my attention back to my screen where I have incoming intelligence reports popping up every few minutes, labelled green. Green means nothing serious, orange means a low level threat, red means something serious is happening, and black, well, I suppose that would equate to a full-blown war, but we've just had one of those so I don't expect to see black reports any time soon.

Kohler leans over my shoulder and whispers into my ear, "I don't think I'll discipline Harold, it's good to know that you're all alone up here." His lips brush against my ear. I taste bile.

"I'm just doing my job, sir." I keep my tone steady, not wanting to lead him on and not wanting him to know he's intimidating me.

He runs his finger down my cheek. "Good girl. Maybe if you're really good I will reconsider your punishment."

I lower my eyes; I don't like where the conversation is going.

"We'll talk about this tomorrow; it's too hot for any real *discussions* tonight."

I shiver involuntarily.

Kohler leaves and Luca comes out of the server room looking like he's been roasted. "That guy is a creep." His agitation is making him flex his muscles, like he's ready to pounce.

"Yeah, well, he's a Crone. What do you expect?"

Luca begins pacing. "What's he planning on doing tomorrow night?"

My stomach clenches. I know exactly what he's planning; I saw it in his eyes — the hunger.

"I dunno; make me input data or something equally as boring."

Luca turns and glares at me. "Cass, you know as well as I do what he's thinking."

I stand up and walk over to Luca. "Luc, stop worrying, I can take care of myself." I put my clammy hand in his sweaty one. "I can handle Kohler."

Luca sighs and shakes his head. "I don't like this."

"You'd better go before someone finds you here."

Reluctantly he leaves and I stand alone, with a sleeping Harold nearby, dreading tomorrow.

Much later I get into bed just as the boys are getting up. Luca turns on his side in his bed and looks at me. "I still don't like this."

"There's nothing you can do — you're on duty tonight aren't you? Stop worrying, I promise I can take care of myself."

He clenches his pillow, then gets up and pads moodily to the bathroom. Simon watches him go. "What's got into him?"

I roll my eyes. "Nothing, he's just overreacting about something."

"About what?"

I let out an exaggerated sigh. "Kohler was being a creep last night; Luca thinks he's going to try something."

Simon looks at me earnestly. "Really? You think he will?"

I shrug.

"Cassia, that's really serious, is the Major around? You should talk to him."

"He's not, he's never here, you know that. Look, it's fine, I'll take care of it."

Simon frowns. "Well, if you need us, for anything, we'll be there for you Cass."

"I know you will. Thank you."

I lie down and allow my worry to wash me away into sleep. I wake up at four, my body drenched in sweat. The air is still and heavy. I feel like I'm suffocating. I go down to the gym, the only place with air conditioning, and work out until my muscles are trembling and useless. I join the others for supper later that day, enjoying the distraction of their idle banter. With heavy feet I make my way to work and watch with nervous anticipation as Harold settles down to sleep on the sofa.

At ten o'clock I notice commotion on one of the streets, a group of about twenty people arguing with two guards. I radio in the threat and I am told that I'll need to go in as backup as I'm the closest. I take a gun from the cabinet and put it in a belt holster. When I reach Street 32 things have begun to escalate fast — the group of civilians are yelling at the soldiers about their treatment of one of their friends. It seems he was out after curfew and had been beaten; the man is sitting on the ground clutching his head, his eye already swollen and blood is sliding down the side of his face. I don't know what to do. I agree with them; he shouldn't have been assaulted by the soldiers.

"Does he need medical attention?" I ask.

"What do you care?!" a woman spits.

"I care; I want to make sure he's going to be okay. Sir, are you badly injured?"

"I — I think my arm might be broken," he replies weakly.

I shoot the soldiers a filthy look.

"Okay, I'll take you to the medical centre and everyone else can go back to their homes."

Apparently this is the wrong thing to say. They begin shouting in outrage that justice won't be done and the soldiers will just get away with it. I try to calm them, but they're yelling and screaming and a man in his thirties picks up a rock and is about to throw it at one of the soldiers who is holding a rifle and looks pretty keen to use it.

"Sir, put the rock down!" I yell. He ignores me. If I don't act quickly the situation will spiral out of control.

"Sir, I said to put the rock down." I draw my weapon. A man steps out from behind him, out of the shadows, a man I recognise. He was my great-aunt's old neighbour. He used to help her with her shopping and small jobs around the house.

"Cassia?" He looks at me with so much hurt. "Cassia, this is my grandson."

"Roger, I need him to put the rock down. If he doesn't, things are going to go downhill really fast." People are still yelling and I can hear the pounding of running footsteps; backup is arriving.

"But, can't you see what they've done?"

"Roger, please." I'm in an impossible situation. I don't want to hurt either of them but if I don't do something then there's likely to be a full-blown riot. Already people are beginning to leave their homes to see what's happening. I have to stop it. Also, if I don't act like a Crone I could put myself in a really bad position. I need to be able to keep looking into ways to free my dad, and I haven't even begun to come up with a feasible plan.

"Sir, last warning. Put. The. Rock. Down."

He draws back his arm, and I fire.

I've made the decision before I pull the trigger. I have to — it's the only way to stop my hands from shaking so that I can make a clean shot. I twist my body so that the shot will only hit the man holding the rock; I can't risk hurting anyone else. I let out a breath as he pulls back his arm, and I press the trigger. I make the choice not to fire a warning shot; if I missed then it would escalate the situation, but by hitting him, I hope it will make them realise we are serious.

He screams in pain and surprise. I will never forget that scream.

The shot is clean through and through. I hope I've missed bone but it's dark and I'm not the best shot, even at such close range. He grips his arm in agony. The crowd quietens down in shock and fear. They know now that we're serious. Captain Fleming shows up and instructs two different soldiers to take the wounded to the surgery, and the rest encourage the crowd to disperse. I feel disgusted with myself — I've just shot a man for holding a rock. Captain Fleming gives me a nod of approval and sends me back to my post. As I turn to leave I catch Simon's eye; he looks away.

I am completely on edge when I get back to my desk. I can't risk investigating the GDO; I'm sure to make a mistake. I watch as reports systematically update — it's hypnotic and helps steady my heart rate.

At 1:30am I hear footsteps. I hold my breath; I've forgotten Kohler's threat in the chaos. A hand rests on my shoulder and, holding back a shiver, I turn to see Jono.

"Jono? What are you doing here?" I wipe my palms on my trousers.

"I had a break and so came to see how you were doing." He's looking sheepish.

"Did Simon tell you what happened?"

"Kohler's been here?"

"No. Outside, earlier?"

"No. I came to see if I had to come kick that creep in the bollocks."

"Oh! That's really sweet of you." I'm touched by his chivalry.

"We all look out for each other; you'd do the same of us, right?"

I smile. "Is someone being sexually aggressive towards you? Do you want to talk about it?"

Jono grins. "Yeah, Drummer. That guy puts me on edge."

"Does he mind that you tease him so much about his sexuality? I mean, isn't it, well, wrong?"

"I've known him since we were thirteen, we're practically brothers so everything is fair game. Including my gorgeous self."

We start laughing but we're interrupted by someone at the door — Kohler.

I clear my throat. "Good evening, sir."

"What's all this?"

"Evening report, sir. There was suspicion of someone near the perimeter but turned out to be a stray dog." I keep my voice steady to hide the lie.

"I'll be getting back to my post." Jono turns to give me a meaningful look before he leaves. I set my jaw; I won't let Kohler get the better of me.

"Fortis, will you come to my office for a moment, I need to talk over this evening's events."

He speaks formally to the room, just in case Harold is awake. I follow him down the hall into his office; my heart is pounding so hard I'm sure he can hear it. He closes the door behind me and for the first time in my life I feel claustrophobic, trapped.

He moves towards his desk and then hesitates, turning to me. I clench my fists to hide their trembling. My eyes scan the room for a weapon, but instead of finding what I want, I see a hard drive on his desk.

"Fortis, you owe me a great deal for the embarrassment you have caused me, although your actions tonight were swift and effective, which somewhat improves my estimation of you in more ways than one." He steps closer; too close. His breath is on my face; the smell of his sweat fills my nostrils, sickly sweet and bitter at the same time. He hitches his belt.

I look directly at him. He can easily overpower me. I'm on my own; no one can come to my rescue. Think. Think…

"Sir, do you know how old I am?" It's not a question he is expecting. I can see he wants me to whimper and submit to him. "Seventeen."

He seems a little taken aback. "I thought you were at least eighteen."

"No, sir. Are you aware that a seventeen-year-old is considered underage in this country? I would imagine that that's something the GDO would agree with, don't you?" I can see his hesitation.

"Even if an act were consensual, it would still be deemed... inappropriate." I look meaningfully at the red light on the security camera and he steps back, out of my personal space. He turns towards his desk and runs his index finger along it, past the hard drive that I need. "For a man in your position it's too high a risk."

He looks up at me. "Are you threatening me?"

"Consensual or not, *sir*, if someone were to find out, it would be the end of your career."

Then he's right up against me again, holding my face in his hand. His grip is so tight I think my jaw will break.

"Do not threaten me, Fortis."

Through clenched teeth I manage a reply. "No, sir, don't threaten *me*."

He pushes me up against the door, his eyes wild, his body quivering. He's panting and I feel myself begin to really panic. I am powerless against him; he's twice my size and filled with anger. I won't be able to fight him off. His hand goes to my neck and begins to choke me as he unbuckles his belt.

My throat is burning, but his grip loosens slightly as he's preparing himself.

I manage to choke out, "Do you know what they do to paedophiles in prison?"

He pauses.

"Do you know what the GDO does to them?" It's a gamble. I don't know what the GDO would do but I'm pretty sure it can't be good. They do like to punish people, after all. I can finally see genuine fear in his eyes. He lets go of me and unlocks the door. I make to leave but he stops me by grabbing my hair and holding me to the spot.

"This isn't over, Fortis."

He forces me to turn around and throws me against his desk, his name plaque slamming into my chest, causing me to gasp in pain. Still holding my hair, he bends down and whispers into my ear, "And you will like it." Finally, he lets go of me and turns to the door. I grab the hard drive and quickly tuck it into the waistband of my trousers.

I walk out of his office calmly and slowly, make my way to the bathroom, and then throw up violently into the toilet. Shaking, I rinse my mouth out and open the door and nearly have a heart attack when I see someone was standing behind it — it's Jono, looking haunted.

"You okay?" I nod. "I, uh, hid behind the hall filing cabinet and I was about to come in Cass, I was going to stop him, I promise."

I find my voice, even though it's weak after being sick and being choked. "It's good you didn't, it would have made things worse."

Jono's voice is hollow. "I should have come in."

"No, you did the right thing. Thank you for looking out for me."

Jono looks down. "I should have stopped all of that."

"Nothing happened." Nausea swims through me again.

"Cassia, what just happened wasn't nothing. We're all going to make sure that nothing like that happens again. I don't want to hear any brave nonsense from you — we're not letting that creep anywhere near you again." Jono pulls me into a hug and I can feel his heart hammering; he's almost as scared as I am. We're really just kids still.

"Okay. Thank you." I can't argue; I don't have the strength.

I sit alone at my desk for the rest of the night with Harold asleep behind me, barely more than part of the furniture. I swear to myself that if Kohler comes near me again I won't think twice about acting in self-defence.

Before I leave for the night, I pretend I've dropped something and then I hide the hard drive in a loose panel below my desk. I'll use it when I can think clearly again.

When I get into the dorm in the morning, after I've scrubbed my skin raw, the boys are all still awake but they're silent, wary. I can't look at them. I feel shame, even though I've done nothing wrong with Kohler, but I also feel disgusted with myself for shooting Roger's grandson. I get into bed and pull my covers high. I hear Luca get out of bed and climb in behind me. He wraps his big arms around me and I allow tears to tumble down my cheeks until I fall asleep — finally feeling protected.

I wake up safe and comforted in Luca's arms. I shift slightly, trying not to wake him, but he's on alert and wakes up instantly. He looks around before he looks at me, my protector. He squeezes me tight and kisses my cheek.

"Thanks for staying with me."

"Any time, soldier."

The others are stirring. One by one they prop themselves up and look in my direction. Drummer is the first to break the silence.

"Jono told us about last night."

"I handled it." My voice doesn't hold the conviction I am trying to portray.

"But your excuse will only buy you time. Cass, you're eighteen in two months."

I look at Luca, trying to tell him that I don't intend for us to stay that long. I can't keep being a Crone.

"We need to do something about him." Jono is looking uncomfortable; he's feeling bad for not helping me out.

"If we do that we'll be kicked out of the army, or worse, and we don't want that." I'm pleading with them; I don't want to think about the previous night ever again.

Simon is looking at me warily. "Simon, did you tell them about what happened?" I speak in an almost whisper. He looks away from me and I feel such deep shame that I'm sure my insides have become hollow.

I look at Luca, barely able to confess even to him. "I — I shot someone last night."

"What? Who?" Luca looks at me in shock. I explain what happened, and as I do I can feel the warmth of Luca's body drawing away. I've never felt so alone.

"I had to arrest a woman three days ago." Jono catches my eye and then looks away. "She'd stolen food vouchers because her children were always hungry. I had to escort her to a prison cell as she sobbed for her children because there was no one to take care of them."

I turn to Luca, "What would you have done?"

"I wouldn't have shot him."

My stomach drops.

"I wouldn't have been able to make the hard decision Cass, I'd have hesitated and then there would have been a full-blown riot. You're stronger than I am."

I let out a gasping sob and shake my head and then try to speak, but can't. The demons of the previous night are wrapped around me and suffocating.

"I mean it, you did the right thing."

If that's the case, then why is he sitting so far away? Drummer shoots Luca a loaded look and comes over to me and wraps me in his skinny arms.

"Last night was the shittiest." Drummer kisses the top of my head.

"Yeah, it was."

"Being in the army isn't as glorious as I'd thought it'd be," Jono sighs.

"Who gives a shit about the GDO army?" I am surprised that it's Simon who said it and not one of the others. We all look around warily; there's a strong chance that our room is bugged.

"I do." I look to Luca; we have to keep up our pretence, even if now he wants to distance himself from me.

Jono and Drummer give each other a knowing look.

"What?" Luca is picking up on something unsaid.

"Well, I mean, do any of us really like the GDO, apart from, you know, the obvious people — Kohler, for one?" Drummer is cautious — he speaks so quietly it's hard to hear exactly what he's said, knowing that if any of us disagree he'll be reported and court-martialled.

"Maybe we should have this conversation elsewhere…" Luca taps his ear.

We sit in a circle on the floor in the bathroom with the showers on — if the room is bugged they won't be able to hear what we're saying; well, we hope anyway. We've all seen it in films at any rate.

"What are you trying to say, Drummer?" Luca is still wary. If either one of us shows our distaste for the GDO, we'll definitely land both of us in it.

"I mean, come on, they're a bunch of wankers."

I can't help but smile. Simon and Jono nod in agreement.

"Yeah, they're massive twats, it's not like anyone can do anything about it," Simon responds.

"So, how come you guys joined up then?" I'm still not ready to blow our cover.

"When the war ended we decided that if we joined up it wouldn't matter 'cos we wouldn't be shooting people, you know? Pays good, foods better than anywhere else, get to play with guns, there's running water and a bed. Drummer would be in his equivalent of the Playboy mansion; doesn't mean you have to like your boss just because you work for them."

"There was just nothing else for us…" Drummer seems ashamed.

"And you, Simon?"

"It was the right option at the time." We fall silent. All of us are here as a last resort.

"What about you two?" Jono looks at us, interested. I am still too nervous to reveal our true intentions — none of them have decided to be out and out spies.

"Well… we…" I can't find a way to explain it. I look to Luca.

"We wanted to do something…" Luca is hesitant to reveal my intentions.

I take a breath. "I want to free my dad."

"Your dad?" Simon furrows his brow. I sigh, and reluctantly explain.

"My dad's a prisoner here, a political prisoner. I wanted to try and get him out and, well, I thought if I was in the GDO I could, you know, find out stuff about them that showed their weaknesses."

I blush. I am embarrassed by my scheme. I feel young and foolish. I didn't really think it through; I didn't consider the actions I would have to take as a soldier, but it's too late to change course. I'm in the army and I have to do what I can and quickly, because I'm not sure I can make another critical decision like the one I'd made the night before.

"Makes sense to me. If I had family left, I'd do the same." Drummer is deadpan; he really means it.

"Kohler suspects though," I reply.

Luca turns to me in shock. "You didn't tell me that."

"Why do you think he's so interested in me? It's not just because I'm the only girl in his department."

Luca grinds his teeth.

"So, what you got so far?" Simon leans forward, ignoring Luca's tension.

Feeling a little more confident I explain. "I hacked some files, haven't had a chance to really look at them yet though, I've put them somewhere safe."

"What can we do to help?" Jono is unsuccessfully trying to hide his eagerness. I realise that maybe the army's appeal has just risen again.

Luca smiles. "Looks like we've got ourselves a squad, Cass."

I smile back, relieved. It's good to have more people on our side, even if two of them are reckless and one resentful. Our plan is beginning to feel a *little* more achievable.

That night, Simon's on the lookout for Kohler whilst I download everything I'd found in the database in Utonia. He's standing in front of one of the security cameras; if he fakes a sneeze then Kohler is on his way. The camera is looped back an hour, and Harold is sound asleep as I make the transfer — it'll take forty-five minutes. I watch carefully as the download counts down. After thirty minutes a cat crosses Simon's path and he starts sneezing uncontrollably. I am about to cancel the download when he looks up to the sky and mouths, "Damned cat." Allergies. I start breathing again and let the transfer continue, my ears pricked in anticipation of any noise, my eyes dried out from staring at the monitor that shows Simon.

The download is complete. Calmed, I unplug the hard drive and put it back in its hiding place. Kohler doesn't show up that night. We have the information, and now we need to get it away from the GDO so we can decide what to do with it. It's time to figure out a way of helping my dad escape. I've already decided how to disable the computer system — all we have to do is find a way of breaking in, and out, of the prison.

I don't see Kohler again during any of my night shifts but I don't feel reassured; he's biding his time, thinking of a way of taking me down. I struggle with sleep, not just because of the threat of Kohler looming over me, but also the look on Roger's face as he cradled his grandson keeps cutting through me, leaving me feeling like I'm drowning.

On Sunday, along with Luca and a few others, I make the trip into Amphora to see my mum. She has a lot more energy, which means it's time to see if I can get her transferred. I don't tell her what has been happening but just being with her make things feel… less. Originally I planned to use Kohler's attraction to me to my advantage to get Mum assigned to Camburg, but I'm too scared to encourage him further. I'm going to have to take a different route. Feeling better than I have in days, I head to Luca's house to see his parents but I make a quick stop along the way.

Clive's place is a hidden basement in his parents' old house — he draws power from a nearby GDO house and runs his computers through their terminals. I go in through the back entrance in the garden where there's a small wooden hatch. Nothing seems different; it was always the way into his computer lair. His mum used to bring us homemade cookies and hot chocolate and never seemed to mind that her son was into illegal activities.

Before I've even walked into the room, Clive greets me.

"How'd you know it was me?" He points to the ceiling. There are cameras dotted around. "You have more surveillance in here than the GDO spying on a Resistance meeting."

"What brings you here?"

"I need a virus." I sit down next to him and stare at his monitors.

"That I can do. What for?" He rubs his eyes; he's spending too much time in the dark.

"I've found a way into the GDO mainframe in Utonia."

His mouth falls open — he wasn't expecting that. "H-how?"

"I have access to their computers. Everything is connected."

Clive shakes his head. "Amateurs."

"I know, right?"

"So, what do you want this virus to do?" He turns back to his desk and starts rifling through USB drives.

"I know how to bring the local system down but I need it to stay down to buy me some time. I also need a virus to plant in the Utonia system — I've pulled off some data from there but I haven't had a chance to look at it."

Clive's face lights up. "Can I have a look?" I give him the details of the drop box.

"Maybe you can make sense of it for me. I've also got a hard drive copy, as backup."

"Good idea, you never know if they'll find out we're piggy-backing off their Internet service." Clive stretches. "Mum should be back with some food soon — want to stay?"

"Wish I could, but I have to be going. How is your mum?"

Clive smiles. "Really enjoying her secret new life, she was always an anarchist at heart. So, how are you going to bring down their system?"

"The server room, there's an overheating problem."

"Clever. I have the perfect virus. If you install it and then let the system crash, it'll make it look like the overheating caused damage to the system. It'll take them hours to restore it." He hands me a USB drive. "It works fast so once you upload it, get the hell out of there."

"Perfect! Clive, you quite literally are a life saver."

Despite the blue reflection from his screens, I can see his blush. "Maybe you should get some sun though, can't be good for you being cooped up in the dark."

He stands up and stretches his legs. "Can't afford to be caught, I'm registered as deceased."

I laugh and gave him a hug. "You were always the smartest person I know. Thanks for this; you have no idea how much it'll help. Be safe."

"You too."

The sun makes black spots dance in front of my eyes when I emerge from the basement. I tuck the USB drive into my bra and head to Luca's house. I'm greeted with warm hugs and warm smiles by his parents, but Ellyas is nowhere to be found.

WEEK NINE

I'm finally back to normal working hours, but my sleeping patterns have been messed up from night shifts and so I can't seem to sleep properly. At 4am I give up and go to the gym. Halfway through my workout I go to get a drink and catch my reflection in the mirror; I am already starting to look leaner. I'm finally getting stronger, which gives me some confidence. If I keep working out I won't feel so vulnerable around Kohler any more.

The boys and I have an early morning conference in the shower room to discuss how we're going to rescue Dad, and I fill them in on the first stages of the plan. Simon is still a little off and I'm not sure how reliable he's going to be. Jono and Drummer's enthusiasm is great, but I worry that they don't see how important getting the plan right is. I just hope we have a fully committed team.

With the security system down along with the computers, we will be able to move about undetected and other GDO stations won't be alerted straight away. It will buy us some time. Simon is in charge of looking for a safe haven for when we get out because he's come across a stash of maps in a guard station. Luca says he'll talk to Shreya about the prison to see if he can get any information out of her. I ignore the knot in my stomach when he mentions her name.

We'll all do what we can to assess the prison and I'm tasked with trying to find some blueprints. Once again, I have no idea where to start. The old library or town hall is my best bet, but how do I do the research without arousing suspicion?

I'm lucky enough to be working with Jaidee again; he seems to know everything about the way the GDO is run, and about Camburg.

"Jaidee, how do we know where our perimeter lies in a town like this?"

"Well, when we moved in here we looked at the old town plans and marked out our borders, keeping all essential buildings within those parameters." His reply is immediate and off-hand; I haven't alerted suspicion, yet.

"So what, the school, the surgery, the prison, the library, the police station…" I keep my tone nonchalant.

"And the town hall."

"Lucky you found the plans."

Jaidee taps away at his computer. "The library has archives of the town plans and blueprints for all the buildings, it wasn't hard to find them in the basement."

"Were there any cool old books down there?"

Jaidee looks at me; he can barely hide his excitement. "Well, I did find a copy of Victor Hugo's *Les Contemplations*, which I think could be a first edition."

"Really? Wow, that's incredible." I try to match his enthusiasm, whatever the book is.

"I know, it's a real find, I might go back there and take a look to see what else is down there."

"Can I come? I'd love to help you rummage. Wait, are we allowed down there?" I bite my lip; I want Jaidee to think I'm afraid of going against the GDO.

"Of course we can, it's not a problem at all. Hey, I know, I'll take you down at lunch."

"Wow, thanks Jaidee, that's really cool of you."

Jaidee and I take our sandwiches to the library with us as we sift through piles of dusty old books. Whilst Jaidee's completely engrossed I get up to look around. At the back of the room I find drawers of plans, but despite searching I can't find one of the prison, which I suppose makes sense — you wouldn't have plans for a prison just lying about. Feeling deflated I make my way back to Jaidee, glancing at the stacks as I go. I pause in the architecture section, an idea fluttering in my brain. I go back to Jaidee with an armful of books.

"What you got there?"

"I've always been interested in architecture, wanted to be an architect, you know, before." Jaidee nods solemnly.

"Anyway, I thought I could look into the architecture of this town, have a little project."

"Actually, I know the place quite well I could give you a tour, talk you through some of it." He is puffed up with pride; I can't help but like him, especially because of his willingness to help.

Matching his earlier excitement, I ask, "Can we go after work?" One enthusiast to another.

That afternoon Jaidee takes me on a tour of the town, explaining the important buildings to me. Eventually we reach the prison.

"Now, the prison is interesting as it was actually an old monastery." Jaidee's eyes are gleaming with pride — he really does know a lot about Camburg.

"Really, how interesting, when was it converted?"

"About eighty years ago. The town was growing and it's a good distance from Amphora." I nod in response. "The layout inside is pretty interesting, it still has a courtyard and the old arches."

"You can hardly tell from out here, how on earth did you get to see inside?"

Jaidee looks embarrassed. "I didn't, there are some photos in the archives."

"Wow, I'd like to see them."

Jaidee leads me rear to the library. At the back of the archives he shows me to an old cabinet. Inside is a folder with photos of the monastery before and after its transformation — it's not a blueprint, but I think I can figure out a basic layout from them.

When Jaidee goes to the toilet I take the relevant photos with me, and that night I sit with the boys and we cobble together a rudimentary plan for the prison.

"Look over here." Simon is pointing at an old photo of the monastery outer wall.

"I don't see anything — it's just a wall, mate." Drummer rubs his eyes; it's getting late.

"Not the wall, there — in the grounds in front. That looks like a hatch."

"Like a tunnel into the monastery?" I look at him, unable to contain my excitement.

Luca considers it. "Maybe, but Cassia, you know that it's most likely been blocked off when they built the prison."

"Possibly, but if the tunnel still exists, couldn't we unblock it?"

Simon shrugs. "We'll have to investigate."

Luca looks up at me and gives me a half smile. "Fancy a run tomorrow, Fortis?"

Luca and I get up early for our run; the humidity means there's usually a thick fog first thing. We grab a banana each before we set off and take our time stretching to help our bodies wake up. We start off slowly, allowing the warmth to get into our muscles and loosen them. The air is dense in our lungs. Once we reach the woods we immediately turn left and make our way towards the prison. The trees clear just before the prison wall — fortunately, with the heavy morning haze we are still cloaked from the cameras. We crawl forward and, using markers memorised from the photos, find our way to the spot where the tunnel should have been, but there's nothing there.

"Shit."

"Don't give up yet."

Luca feels around the surrounding area, searching for something to signify the entrance. He stops, taps lightly on the ground, and then searches around for edges. He nods at me and I crawl over and help him try and lift the wooden board. The wood is old and rotting and splinters when we finally haul it back. I look around to see if the cracking of decaying timber has alerted anyone to our presence, but it hasn't. We get our torches out and shine them into the hole. Aside from a few creepy-crawlies it seems to be intact, as far as we can see. Carefully we lower ourselves down and close the hatch behind us. Slowly we walk through the damp and surprisingly cool tunnel. It smells of earth and moss. After a while we come to a dead end.

"Do you think we're at the prison wall?" I whisper. Luca nods and gently taps on the wall with the back of his torch. He frowns; the wall's thick. I shine my torch around the edges. Nothing. I focus on the brickwork to see if there are any loose bricks, but I can't see any. I sigh and run my hand along the wall. As I do, some of the cement crumbles under my fingers. I brush my finger along the seam between the bricks, and the mortar comes away easily.

"What the…?" Luca helps me brush the cement around a brick, and with my small fingers we manage to loosen and then pull the brick out. I look at the dust on my hands and then at the cement around the rest of the wall.

"This is different stuff; someone's been through here before."

"Must have been a prison break or a bad patch up job. Let's see how many we can get out." We manage to remove a layer of bricks big enough for Luca to crawl through; behind them is another layer. I shine my torch on my watch; it's 6am.

"Luc, we need to get going, the fog will clear soon." We pile the bricks up and head back. At the end of the tunnel Luca brushes past me and I immediately get goose bumps. Now is hardly the time to be thinking about him like that, I berate myself. Luca carefully peers out and then helps me up. We make sure the hatch remains covered and then run to the lake to wash off the cement dust. Being back at the lake with Luca reminds me of the last time we'd been there together, and I find it hard to look at him. I concentrate on getting myself clean. I just wish I could keep my focus on more pressing concerns, like espionage.

"We should get back."

"Wait a second." Luca is looking at me intently, and my heart stutters. He comes towards me and brushes tunnel crap from my hair. I find it hard to hide my disappointment. I've forgotten that things have changed since the night I pulled my gun on a civilian. The thought of it makes me feel sick, so I imagine he feels the same.

"Oh, thanks."

"No problem." He looks at me for a time-stopping moment and then says we should get back.

I run harder than I had intended back to Camburg; I want to pound out my frustration. Is Luca really that upset with me? There is something wrong with the world if I can figure out what a slime ball like Kohler wants from me, but I can't tell, at all, what Luca wants. Maybe it isn't the world; maybe I am just too confused by my own feelings.

Back in the Intelligence building I allow the monotony of work to distract me. When Claude and Elliot head out for a late lunch I decide to investigate the server room further. My top is already sticking to me from the heat, but I have to take the opportunity when I can. When I open the door I feel choked by the temperature inside. Groaning to myself I plunge in. On the back wall an air-conditioning unit splutters out a breath of tepid air. It's completely ineffectual. Covering my hand with a discarded cleaning cloth, I inspect the unit and take note of the heating settings; it will be easy to make it look like the machinery overheated without leaving any evidence. No one ever wants to enter the server room anyway.

I wash my face in the sink to try and cool myself down and splash the back of my neck. I've never found the climate in Auria so unbearable before. My head swims from dehydration, so I begin to gulp down glasses of water from the cooler; halfway through my fourth glass, Kohler interrupts me. I wipe my mouth and stand to attention, grateful my unease can be mistaken for my discomfort in the oppressive heat. The sight of him sickens me but I manage to control my gag reflex and speak first. "Is there anything I can do for you, sir?"

Kohler looks at me for a beat, a bead of sweat trickling down his forehead. With his index finger he flicks it away. "Not right now, Fortis."

I don't miss the threat but I also don't give it time to linger in the air to increase in force; instead, I take the opportunity. "In that case, sir, might I ask a favour?"

"A favour?" It's not the response he's expecting; I suspect he wants to see me quake.

"My mother is an experienced nurse; she's been unwell but is ready to return to work. I thought maybe the doctor's surgery here could do with some assistance?"

"What on earth makes you think I'll grant you the privilege of a favour?" His eye contact doesn't waver, but neither does mine.

"Let's just say I was very generous when I chose not to speak to the Major..."

"Are you blackmailing me?" His face darkens. I try to stay calm.

"Just a favour, sir. I would then, of course, be in your debt." I am playing a dangerous game, one I'd promised myself I wouldn't enter into. I know that, but it's my best chance of getting my mum close by, and she has to be if we're going to help Dad escape.

Kohler adjusts his belt and leers down at me. "Very well, Fortis, I'll grant you this favour but if I choose to collect soon, that will not be a problem. Understood?"

"Yes, sir."

"Interesting that you should want your mother nearby as well." He gives me a loaded look.

I don't move from where I'm standing until he's gone. I've just put myself in a very precarious position; I have to do something about Kohler. I walk slowly back to my computer and begin to think over my options.

We take it in turns to go in pairs to widen the tunnel to the prison; by the end of the week we've made significant progress. Drummer and Jono are the ones to reach the locked door, which, unsurprisingly, they have no problem unlocking. They risk a peek through the door and confirm that it opens onto a hallway just off the central yard. With our exit from the prison secured, we just have to decide on our plan to get in and out with the prisoners.

We're sitting on the cool bathroom tiles late on Sunday night, discussing our next steps with the showers raining down behind us, when we come up with another stage of our plan.

"So, how do we actually pull off a jail break? I mean really, this is kind of out of our league, don't you think?" Simon is fidgeting as he speaks, afraid of our judgement.

"Look, I know this is dangerous and this is completely my fight, not yours, so, I understand if you want to pull out." I pause and look around. "If *any* of you want to." I look purposefully at Luca.

There is silence in the group as they all take a moment to look around themselves.

"I don't want to pull out; I just don't know how we'll pull it off…" Simon looks intently at one of the cracked tiles.

Luca takes charge. "Okay, so here's how I see it going… Cassia plants the virus and sets the server to overheat. How long will that give us?"

"Hard to say, they won't come back online easily after that — I'd say minimum one hour."

"Okay, so that's our window. We have an hour to break everyone out. So, I guess we'll know when the system is down?" Luca looks to me.

"All security systems will be down, they will lock down though, so any doors we need to get through will need to be opened somehow." I glance at Jono.

"Bit of brute force should do it — Drummer has a crowbar stashed under his bed, should work."

No one bothers asking why Drummer has a crowbar.

"Okay, so then we can gain entry into the prison. Shreya mentioned that there are five guards on duty at all times. I think early morning would be the best time to strike." Everyone nods in agreement with Luca. "I'm thinking 3am — it's when you feel like you're dead on your feet — the guards should be easier to overpower."

"What about shift rotations?" I ask.

"Good point — can you find them out Cass?" I tell them that I can.

"Wait, what about the prison's backup generator? I mean, there must be one otherwise the cell doors would just open every time there was a power cut…"

"We could crowbar that too?" Drummer seems so casual about the task that it's almost funny.

"Is that dangerous?" Simon looks to me; not that I have a clue.

"Uh, I don't know. Guys, just don't electrocute yourselves… look for a switch or plug, or something. I'll see if I can find out anything on the ones we use." I am starting to wish we had someone with actual military training to help us.

"Right, okay, so, we kill the security systems, take out the generator, which we need to find first, open the doors and then confront the guards…" The look on Luca's face is enough; we don't want to have to confront other people. What if someone got hurt?

Drummer sits up straighter. "What if they start a riot?"

"A riot?" I look at him sceptically.

"Yeah. If the prisoners overpower the guards from the inside when we enter, we can just lead them out." Drummer has a point.

"It's a good idea, but how do we get them to riot?" We all sit in silence; I can almost hear Drummer and Jono trying to think.

"I need to find a way to get a message to my dad." Reluctantly I turn to Luca. I know how to get that message to him but I just don't like how it would have to come about. "Luc, can you get closer to Shreya? You have to get her to show you around. You know Dad, you'll recognise him and you can slip him a note from me." The others shift uncomfortably as Luca looks at me intently.

"If that's the plan then I'll do it."

I nod and look away; my stomach feels like it's filled with writhing snakes. We all know what he has to do and it's not like Luc and I are together or anything, but it doesn't stop me feeling miserable. Once again, I don't sleep well.

WEEK TEN

Nearly everything is in place. We just have to figure out when we are going to make our big escape and where exactly we're going to go. Simon has been looking into possible locations and says that he has a few options, but wants to do more research before he decides. But, before we go ahead I have to make another trip to Amphora to see Clive to collect the virus to infect Utonia's mainframe. I am surprised when the opportunity comes sooner than I'd anticipated.

As I suck on my morning ice-cube, Kohler strides purposefully into the computer room.

"Fortis, you're to go to Amphora today."

"Sir?" My heart pounds. Had he really come through for me?

"You're to collect some supplies and we have a new nurse who will need escorting back."

I hold back my excitement. "Yes, sir."

The look on his face means that he has something planned, that this is somehow going to make things worse for me, but I don't care. My mum will be close by; I can reunite my parents.

By eleven o'clock I'm back in Amphora. The truck drops me off and I am to be collected late that afternoon. I have some time before I go to get my mum. I go to see Mena first; I miss her almost as much as I miss my own mother. I have a few supplies with me that Luca has been stashing away for her. She greets me at the door with so much love and warmth that I feel incredibly emotional. She envelopes me in a hug and I hand over the contraband.

"I'm glad I caught you, I thought you might be at the nursery."

"There's a bug going round, the GDO shut it," she shrugs.

"Well, at least it gives you some time off." I hug her again — I can't help myself. I feel so safe with her.

"And how are you coping, little Cassia?" She looks at me with affection.

"Better than I could have imagined, and Luca is looking after me," I smile, and she responds with a knowing nod.

"How are Ellyas and Moses?" Mena busies herself putting away the supplies; she always finds a way to distract herself when she's troubled.

"Moses is well, tired from the long hours but at least he's not doing hard labour like some of our friends. Ellyas... Ellyas is doing fine."

"Mena, what's going on?" Her hands shake slightly as she picks up a cloth to wipe down the kitchen counter.

"Nothing, he's just made new friends, that's all." She looks around, worried. "Actually, he's acquainted with one of your friends."

"One of mine?" I frown, puzzled.

"Yes, Jake."

"Jake?" His name comes out in a hoarse whisper. I understand Mena's countenance then. The last time I saw Jake he was losing it and I knew his anger would make him do something stupid. I have to see him, to make sure he's not being reckless, to make sure he's not dragging Ellyas into something dangerous. I do my best to reassure Mena and give her a fond squeeze goodbye.

Mum is in good spirits; she's sitting up in the chair by her bed and chatting to one of her old colleagues when I enter.

"I'm here to collect you."

She beams at me. "You did it? I'm going to be near you both?"

I sit down next to her and smile. "Yeah, we're going to be together."

My mum lets out a single heartbreaking sob, one that has been held in for months. She holds me close and whispers in my ear, "My brave girl, you're so much like your father."

I leave Mum to sort out her things and collect some clothes. I tell her I'll meet her at the truck in two hours. I have just enough time to collect the virus from Clive, and to try and hunt down Jake.

Fans hum in Clive's lair but the moving air isn't helping cool it down all that much. He hands me the virus with a proud grin.

"My best yet." His brow is glistening from the heat.

"I don't doubt it." I stuff it in my bra and make Clive blush. "So, what's it do?"

"Chews up all their data so that there's nothing left. There's no recovering from this one. You can't rebuild the files once the virus has digested them all, it'll cripple them." He sits back in his chair, puffed with pride.

"How will I release it?"

"Just drag and drop the folder on the USB into the Utonia folder you found, and then open it. Shut everything down and get the hell out of there."

I think for a moment. "What if I load the wrong virus to the wrong place?"

"You won't. I've labelled that one there Black Plague, and the other one is Burnout."

I laugh. Clive loves to label his viruses. "Perfect. Hey, one more question."

"Shoot, soldier." He holds me up with his finger guns.

"Can you find people?"

Clive frowns, "find someone? Who?"

"Jake, he's sort of vanished and I'm worried." I don't want to tell Clive my fears; I don't want to say anything until I'm sure.

"I saw him the other day."

This takes me by surprise; I thought he'd gone underground. "You did?"

"Yeah, brought a smokin' blonde with him." Clive is grinning.

"Yve."

"Yeah, that was her name." His voice turns dreamy.

"What did he want?" I'm agitated now. What is Jake up to and how involved has Yve become?

"Access to surveillance cameras for the old government building."

"GDO headquarters?"

"That's the puppy." He re-cocks his finger guns and fires them at me.

"Oh God." This is a bad sign; a very bad sign.

Clive's expression changes. "What's wrong?"

"Um, nothing, he's just not thinking straight at the moment, you know? Any idea where he is now?" I begin to pace. I have to act quickly; I have to stop whatever he has in motion.

Clive quickly turns to his computers and starts pulling up screens with code and surveillance cameras. After a few minutes he pauses and turns to me.

"He just went into the Hayfair metro station."

"Hayfair?" Of course... of course that's where he'd set up.

We'd found it as kids, an abandoned station that you can access through Hayfair. We'd spent weeks trying to figure out how to pick the lock, and when we did we found old control rooms and tunnels. I would never have done something as risky as breaking in if it hadn't been for Jake encouraging me. I'd have done anything he said back then. Times have changed; I'm not going to let him do something stupid this time.

"One last favour, can you make it so the GDO doesn't see me go in and out?"

"Done."

"Clive, you're a true genius, thank you."

I leave quickly but don't run — running would alert suspicion and I don't want that. It'll take me twenty minutes to get to Hayfair. I move as fast as I can.

The station is relatively busy but not like it was before the GDO arrived. I make my way down the stairs and onto the platform. I slip round the corner, past the control booth and unpick the lock, just like Jake taught me.

It still smells the same, of mould and misuse. I make my way along the corridor until I see the warmth of light, and hear muffled voices. I go straight into the room without even thinking what could be inside. There are five people inside: Jake, Yve, two others, and Ellyas. My heart sinks. There are tables with plans laid out and makeshift bunks around the edges. One of the men I don't recognise looks up and immediately pulls his gun on me.

"How the hell did you find us?" He's nervous; I can tell he's not trained by the way he holds his gun. He won't kill me; he doesn't want to kill. Also, he still has the safety on.

I hold up my hands. "I'm not armed. I'm not here to harm you."

Ellyas and Jake are frozen to the spot.

Yve tuts. "You lot are so paranoid!" She runs up to me and gives me a hug. "Good to see you, how are the Crones treating you?" She brushes her long locks away from her face. She's glowing. She's thriving down in the dark, scheming, rebelling against the system. Yve is more alive than ever, now that she's dancing with danger.

"Oh, you know, a splash of misogyny here, a spot of violence there, the usual."

Her eyes light up, wanting to know more, wanting to get in on any action.

"Who is this?" the gun wielder demands.

"This, dear Robert, is Cassia, she's a woman on the *inside*," Yve says with cocky pride.

Jake approaches me. "What are you doing here, Crone?"

I ignore the insult. "Actually, I came here to ask you the same question." I glare at Jake. He's trying to upset me but it's not going to work. "What are you planning, Jake? Going to attack GDO headquarters? All five of you?"

Ellyas looks at the floor, embarrassed, ashamed.

"As if I would tell a Crone anything." Jake turns his back on me.

"Jake," Yve scolds, and then touches his arm affectionately, intimately. "You're being ridiculous; you know that Cassia isn't a real Crone. Stop being a meathead."

I smile, despite the tension. "This is just like the time I got into the school play and you didn't."

He turns back, disgust on his face.

"It's so like you to make a joke of something like this. So like you to think of yourself, to drag Luca down with you." He steps closer and locks his gaze onto me. "Selfish little Cassia, getting her own way as usual."

His words sting and it takes more self-control than I knew I had to stop myself from punching him. He's found my weak spot, but of course he has, we've been best friends for years. He knows how to make his comments hit hard but then, so do I.

"How's Emma, Jake?"

He freezes, his muscles tense, and the vein in his right temple begins to twitch. It's a low blow but we are all fighting dirty now, it's second nature. He looks away from me, unable to respond, his hand resting menacingly on the gun holstered in his belt.

I look at Ellyas, who can barely meet my eyes. "Luca's doing well. Your mum's worried about you... I saw her today."

"How is she?" Guilt and concern are plain to see; at least Ellyas' conscience seems to be functioning, unlike Jake's.

"You know your mum, nothing can defeat her, except, well, maybe this. Whatever 'this' is..." I allow him time to squirm. I've always looked up to Ellyas; he's intelligent, driven, and I believe him to have strong morals and the sense not to get involved in Jake's mad schemes. Something must have changed.

I step closer, towards Ellyas and away from Jake. The gun is still trained on me as I move.

"Ellyas, go back home, don't get involved." My voice is firm and more commanding than I remember it being.

"Cassia, how can you say that when you dragged my brother with you on your own mission of vengeance?"

I carry on. I have to get through to him, for Ellyas' sake and Luca's.

"We're being smart about it; we're not taking any risks that are too great." I look down and see bomb schematics on the table. For the first time ever I thank the GDO for teaching me a thing or two about weaponry. My pulse is thumping so I take my time and make sure they don't register my panic. I turn to face the rest of them. "What you're planning isn't a rebellion against the regime, it's terrorism. You have to understand that. You have to see that these extreme actions are going to get you and a lot of other people killed. You can't account for the collateral damage for something like this. You need to stop and think about what you're doing." I am pleading, desperate, but I feel like I'm talking to the tide and asking it to stop advancing.

Jake scoffs, "What do you even know? You have no idea what we're planning on doing."

Ellyas shifts uncomfortably, which makes me think that I actually have a very good idea about what they are thinking of doing.

"Be smarter than this, Jake. Using their own tactics against them won't work. They will slaughter thousands to your hundreds, and it will escalate and escalate. It will get out of control very quickly. Please listen to reason; this is not the way to fight them. There are better ways."

"Safer ways, Cassia? Like climbing right into the lion's den? You think *I'm* reckless? Well, you're a bloody idiot. You have no idea what you're doing or who you're up against." He begins to pace with irritation, his mood already too unstable for me to want to stick around for much longer.

"Jake, you're not thinking clearly, none of you are. Bombing the headquarters is suicide."

Jake throws his head back and laughs, the sound chilling me. "Suicide? Well, looks like you're not as stupid as I thought *little* Cassia."

The words choke me, physically constricting my breathing. I gasp for a breath and turn to Ellyas; he responds with only a look of unreachable sadness. I glance at Yve; she's glowing with pride. Jake is glowing with hatred.

"No." I can barely get the words out; they're only a breath. "Please, no." I look around, begging. "Don't do this, please, you have to see, you have to."

Jake looks at Ellyas and he starts to lead me out of the room. I am too stunned to utter another word until we reach the door at the end of the tunnel. I grab Ellyas' arms as tightly as I can. "Don't do this, Ellyas, don't do this to your family. Don't do this to Luca." I can't make him see, but how can I not make him see? He begins to open the door and I beat my fists on his chest and I scream and scream until he holds his hand over my mouth to silence me. I fight him, I kick, and I bite, and I scratch, but he holds me until the fight is gone. I can't struggle against him any longer; my heart is too broken to even try.

I leave the tunnel and make my way onto the platform filled with innocent faces; any one of them could become a victim of their plan. I need to make them understand, somehow, that what they're doing is wrong, that not everyone in the GDO wants to be there. In fact, most of the people I've got to know have only joined because they have no better option, that to bring it down you just have to activate the disease that has already infected its ranks. No organisation can keep going when it's built its foundations with soldiers who are victims of the cause they're told to follow. I just don't know how to get through to them and I don't know how much time I have.

As I reach the road above, a hand touches my shoulder. I spin round to see Yve.

"Cassia, I just… Don't push him away. He's been through too much." It's the first time I've seen Yve look vulnerable, standing there, defending Jake.

"I know, but I can't support this, it's so reckless. You must see that. We're all fighting for the same cause." Pausing, I look around to make sure we we're not being watched. I lower my voice. "I want the same thing as you guys, an end to all of this, but I honestly don't think this is the right way to achieve our goal."

Yve studies my face, thinking. "What's your plan then?"

"We've found a way into their mainframe, we can corrupt their network, cripple them, and then take action, move against them."

Yve smiles. "Cassia, don't you see, you want to move against them, but the only way to do that is with physical force — *violence*."

"There has to be another way." My palms begin to sweat. Is she right? Can we really only achieve our freedom by spilling blood? I don't want that; I have seen too much of that.

"How, Cassia? How?" For the first time that day she looks genuinely serious and I get the sense that she is really asking, that she really wants another solution. Yve doesn't like seeing Jake consumed by revenge either, but she's standing by him anyway. Am I failing him? There are too many questions I can't answer and I am going to be late for my mum. I leave Yve with my head aching.

Mum and the truck are waiting for me when I show up. Mum looks at me as if she knows something is up but she doesn't say anything. She holds my hand the whole way back to the base; it's exactly what I need. Once back in Camburg, I help set her up in her studio flat above the doctor's surgery. It's small, but at least she doesn't have to share with strangers. I take her to collect her food vouchers and some food but have to leave to get my own meal at the barracks; there's not enough food for two in her pack. I feel bad leaving her, but I need to get back and tell the others everything that happened in the capital.

The rhythmic hiss and drum of the water falling has become a faithful companion to all our secret conversations. I lean my cheek against the cool wall tile and close my eyes as the others discuss the information I've just shared. I let their chatter fade into background noise, in cadence with the dancing water.

"When do you think this will happen? Cassia? Cass?" I open my eyes; Luca is talking to me.

"I don't know; it didn't look like they'd built the bomb, not that I saw anyway. They had the schematics out; I doubt they would be laid out if it was already built. But that's just a guess." I sit up straight and face them. "We can't let Jake become a terrorist, we can't let him take innocent lives. The retaliation from an act like that will be — just — just — too enormous to even imagine. I *know* the GDO isn't innocent, but not everyone within their ranks deserves to die."

From the expressions around me I know that they all agree. We are GDO soldiers, and we don't deserve to die because of their crimes. There *are* a few people who are accountable for so much; they're the people that need targeting, and they're the ones who need to be punished. Murder isn't the answer. Murder should never be the answer.

"How big is Jake's network?" Drummer seems unusually deep in thought.

"I don't know, there were only a few people I saw." I see what he's getting at. "We could use his network to take over each town when we disable SINN."

"Exactly," Drummer nods at me.

"The only problem is that they could take things too far. Forceful removal, fine, but how can we be sure they won't execute members of the GDO?" A hush trickles through the room. It's one thing to team up, but there's a lot to consider when your teammates are extremists. The likelihood of us being able to trust them is slim, but the bigger question is whether or not we have a choice because, without them, it's unlikely we can find a way to regain control of our nation.

"Cass, we need to find a way to talk to Jake." Luca is looking at me with something like regret in his eyes; I don't know what it means.

"Yeah, I know, I'll find a way." Sadly, I know that the quickest way is to get another favour from Kohler and I'm already in his debt.

It takes almost a week for me to get to Kohler. I have to get back to Amphora and I can only do it with his permission. I manage to get Luca and I leave to go back for Mena's birthday; we have an entire day. I just can't be sure whether or not Jake will have moved his outfit to a new location. If he's smart he will have, and so there's a strong possibility we'll go looking in the wrong place. We'll have to stop in and see Clive first.

The truck bumps its way to Amphora early in the morning as the fog is dissipating, and the landscape starts to come into view. I remember the drive from years before, where fields stretched as far as the eye could see and small towns and villages peeked out between hills and trees. Now it's a landscape of scars. Houses yawn with mortar holes as a sign of their occupants' resistance; roads are dotted with parked military vehicles; fields churned into mud. Auria is bleeding.

Mena does well to hold back her tears when she sees Luca. I stay only to wish her a happy birthday then leave her alone with her family so I can get the information I need from Clive. As ever he's invaluable, and tracks Jake to our old cleaning haunt in sector H, but he's not working, he's laying low in a boarded up house, probably building a bomb.

"Clive, if you can find him, surely the GDO can too?"

"Jake's careful and I know where to look. The signs that he's there would be missed by anyone else. Besides, I've been covering his tracks."

"Did I ever tell you you're a brilliant genius?"

"Not enough."

I kiss him on his clammy cheek and leave.

I go to collect Luca, and as we say our goodbyes to Mena and Moses she slips something to Luca. I try to ask him what it is but he ignores me. As we walk away it feels like we are saying goodbye forever and the weight of my sorrow fuels my increasing guilt. I have persuaded Luca to give up so much; I am the devil on his shoulder. I am his downfall.

We approach Jake's location with caution. He'll have lookouts, that's for sure, and we want to avoid him running. Luca and I press our backs against the wall of a nearby building and wait for the patrol of GDO soldiers to pass. We're conspicuous in our uniforms and don't want to have our movements noticed. When the coast is clear we make our way carefully down a side alley and climb over a fence into a back garden. We scramble over three more rickety fences before approaching Jake's building. My progress is far less athletic than Luca's.

Richard, the man from the tunnel with the gun, is out in the garden smoking. Pressed together we wait for him to go back inside. Once he's gone we climb the final fence and walk in through the back door, hands raised. We're not armed. We come in peace.

Richard jumps and then scowls when he sees me, and I can tell that he recognises Luca as Ellyas' brother. "Where's Jake?" I'm not in the mood for pleasantries. Richard jerks his head and we follow him into the kitchen.

Jake is leaning over the kitchen island with Yve; they're working on the bomb and it appears to be almost complete. Luca gives me a look that speaks to the hollowness I'm feeling. We wait for Richard to alert them to our presence; we hardly want to alarm someone when they're wrist-deep in explosives.

Jake looks displeased but not surprised when he sees us, whereas Yve beams at us. Luca and I have already agreed that he should speak; the way Jake is reacting to me is hardly going to make him listen to what we have to say.

"Told you there was no point moving, I knew you'd find us again, Cass," Yve says, as she hugs me hello.

Luca nods to her and addresses Jake. "We've been talking a lot this week and we think we've come up with an idea that will have a greater impact on the GDO than your plan."

Jake crosses his arms but doesn't tell Luca to piss off. So far, so good.

"The computer virus that Clive gave Cass can cripple their system and destroy their mainframe, frying all their data. We need to coordinate all the anti-GDO groups in Auria so that everyone can take advantage of their inability to organise troops. They won't even be able to use airstrikes and drones against us; we'd finally have the upper hand."

"So what's your plan? Go in to HQ and bore them to death with your political ideals?" Jake's surliness is bordering on childish. If he hadn't lost so much I'd probably snap at him or kick him in the nuts.

Luca looks at me to explain our plan; reluctantly I begin.

"After I saw you I started thinking, there has to be a better way to take back our territory without killing anyone. So, I was going through their files, trying see if I could get anything out of them that might help, when I came across a folder called Project Eel. The folder had loads of schematics for a new type of electroshock weapon that they were developing for crowd control."

"How does that help us? We can hardly build them all —"

I give Jake my "let me finish" face.

"Turns out the plans were dated from two years ago; they'd decided to stick to water cannons and rubber bullets, as you may remember." Yve winces in recollection. "And then of course, they found that ineffectual and just went back to good old-fashioned bullets. Anyway, I looked into Project Eel some more, and it turns out they did make a batch. A big batch."

Finally, I have Jake's attention. "Well, where are they?"

I look at Luca and smile.

"In Shaanum." Luca pulls out the map and lies it down gingerly next to the bomb. We're both trying to ignore the giant weapon in the room.

"Cass has collected together the guard rotation and security protocols in the area. Now we want to help you guys raid the storage facility, but we'll alert suspicion if we wander off unannounced. This needs to be kept under the radar and we will have to coordinate the raid to the night before we take down their intelligence network." Luca pauses and gives Jake a level look. "We need your help, Jake, we can't do this without you guys, we need you to get those weapons and to rally the other rebels."

Jake looks off into the distance; I can tell he's fighting with himself. He doesn't want to agree to our plan on principle, but he can't deny that it's a good idea. I turn to Yve and nod. She's the only one who can make Jake agree to join us; I just hope it means he'll abandon his own plans.

Yve and Jake head out to the garden together. As I watch them go, Luca reaches out and squeezes my hand. I close my eyes and focus on the comfort that his simple gesture gives me. I open them again when I hear footsteps approaching; as the figure enters the room, Luca releases my hand — Ellyas. He stands, rooted; neither brother is willing to break the tension. I take this as my cue and ask Richard to show me around. I leave the Kemeis to talk whilst I get to know the surly Richard.

There are two more people in the front room; a girl named Alice, and another man named Charlie. They are both from Auria and lost their families and homes in the invasion.

"This is our family, our home now." Alice looks around at the peeling walls and the two men who are under twenty; her only support system. All the new things I learn about the GDO fuels my hatred towards it and strengthens my resolve, but I am still wary about using violence. Even the thought of using the non-lethal guns make my palms sweat, the screams of the man I shot still throbbing in my ears.

"How do you eat if you're not in the system?"

Charlie shrugs in response. "We steal; we have sympathisers who sneak us food. The pain is still so raw here that people are still looking for it to end. I've heard from people from Naevena that after a while people just begin to accept the new way of things; they put their heads down and carry on. They accept their fate. I don't want that to ever happen here."

He becomes more impassioned as he speaks. It's that fire that will drive our rebellion forward but it's also the fire, that if stoked, will destroy everything in its path. We're teetering on the edge of a dangerous mentality. How far we're willing to go for the freedom of our nation is what will define us as revolutionaries or terrorists.

I go back to the kitchen and I'm pleased to see Ellyas and Luca talking civilly.

"Hey, little Cassia." Ellyas gives me a tired smile.

"Hey. I don't suppose you're planning on going back home?"

"He can't, he's on the GDO's list." The list is exactly what it sounds like: a list of names of people who are under suspicion for acts against the regime.

"Ellyas…"

"I know. I'm not going to do anything that would hurt my parents, I see that now. I've just been…" Luca puts his hand on his brother's shoulder, looking wiser, stronger and, surprisingly, older than him.

"We will do what we can to protect you. When we've arranged everything for the prison break we'll let you know the coordinates of our destination."

Ellyas puts his hand on Luca's shoulder and squeezes it.

"We'll need you to bring your parents, and Emma too," I whisper, as I see Jake approaching. Ellyas holds my gaze, telling me he's understood.

Yve and Jake come back into the kitchen. Jake looks resigned and Yve has even more of a glint in her eyes than normal.

Without looking at us, Jake speaks to the room. "Okay, we'll go along with your plan."

I don't stop to think, I just go to him and envelope him in a hug. His body is rigid against mine but I feel him slowly relax before I pull away. I look into his pained eyes and smile. "You're making the right decision, thank you for helping us." He merely nods in response.

Not wanting to push it with Jake, we decide to leave and enjoy the rest of our day off. Jake gives us a pair of encrypted radios; we are to switch them on at quarter past the hour at any hour if we need to contact them.

GDO soldiers aren't allowed to be seen having time off, as it gives the impression that we're lazy and, therefore, weak. But this is our city and Luca and I know just the place to go and eat our rations. When we were cleaners we discovered a lot about our sector. That's why Jake knew about the abandoned house and why we know that there's a hidden underpass that leads to an overgrown community garden. The weeds and plants have completely blocked off any view in or out of this small space, and the main gate is rusted shut.

Luca lays down his shirt for us to sit on. I pull off my boots and shirt and roll up my trouser legs. My tank top and makeshift shorts are far more comfortable than my heavy uniform. I lie back and look up at the blue sky. Luca lies down next to me.

"Lying here, you could almost forget that the world has gone to shit." Luca links his little finger around mine. "I often wonder if there wasn't something that could have been done to prevent all of this."

"You know that there wasn't. At the time the GDO was the best option, until they took things too far." I fix my gaze on the clouds and allow myself to feel like I'm floating along with them. Everything got bad so quickly, unrest here and there, and then suddenly our continent was under martial law.

"Do you think we'll be the last generation to remember what it's like to live in a free nation?" Luca turns to look at me and I pull my eyes away from the sky.

"If you believe that why are you even trying to make a change?" I ask.

"Someone has to."

We lie there in silence until I can't hold in my thoughts any longer. "Luc, do you think you can forgive me ever?"

"Forgive you for what?" He turns to me, perplexed.

"For shooting Malcolm."

"Malcolm?"

"The civilian, on Street 32." I'd looked up his name, it didn't feel right not knowing it after what I did.

"What are you talking about?"

"You've been angry with me since it happened, ever since you heard."

He inches closer. "No, Cass, no." He rubs his face in his hands. "I can't believe you thought that, I would never think that you were to blame. You absolutely made the right decision, the hard decision, but the one that had the best outcome."

"Then what is it?"

"When you told us I realised that I can't protect you and I thought I could. I thought that by being here with you I could keep you safe. First Kohler, and then you had to do something that I know really affected you... I'm not keeping you safe at all."

"I don't need you to keep me safe."

"Yes you do."

"What worries me more is that you feel like you have to carry me and that if I drown, you'll sink alongside me. I don't need to be carried, Luc, I just want someone to be beside me." He frowns. "I shouldn't have let you come."

"Let me?" He's incredulous. "I chose this path."

"No, I forced this path onto you. I made you follow me because *you* wanted to protect me. I've been doing this for me, for my family, I never really considered anyone else." I can feel my throat begin to burn.

"I did it for me too — I don't think I could have sat by and watched as everyone's hope began to fade." He rolls his head away to look at the sky. "Do you know why Ellyas joined Jake?"

"No…"

"He was seeing someone, Lillian, she was…"

"At school with him, I remember her."

"She was killed, but, not just killed, Cass. Four soldiers, they…" He doesn't need to say it. War doesn't just make people kill; it turns them into savages.

"I don't blame him for joining Jake."

"Neither do I."

We lie in silence, thinking of all the misery and horror outside our small sanctuary, knowing that even if we do get our freedom back, nothing, no one, will ever be the same. The damage is irrevocable.

WEEK ELEVEN

Whilst we're away, Simon has found us a location to escape to. After using the GDO's intelligence surveillance system I am able to map out a route to get there, and on Monday evening we do our first active mission against the GDO: we steal supplies.

It's the beginning of our night shift and I'm with Claude in the office. Unfortunately, Claude isn't a napper and so regretfully I lace his coffee with some sleeping pills my mum gave me. I feel guilty bringing her into our schemes in case she gets caught, but I can't risk giving Claude an overdose. At 1am he's in a deep sleep and I rewind the tapes back to 10pm to show the recording of a normal night shift. Fortunately, Kohler is out of town for a couple of days, so I won't be unceremoniously checked up on.

We all meet at the supply warehouse with our packs from training, during the time when it's Jono's scheduled patrol of the area. I disable the alarms easily and switch off the cameras, which reminds me of when I had Yve disable a lock for me — how quickly things have changed. We've agreed to be smart about our stealing and to unload boxes that are further back in the stockroom so no one should, in theory, be alerted.

We fill our packs, reconnect the security system, stash the bags, and go back to our posts. When Claude wakes groggily, at 5am, he apologises. I tell him it's fine but he owes me a sleep one day. He agrees, and nothing more is said. The seamlessness of the operation gives me confidence; maybe we'll be able to pull it off after all.

At 8am the next morning we're back in our shower room talking through the plans for the Shaanum raid.

"I'm just anxious because we won't be there."

Jono elbows me. "Look at Fortis, getting all control freak on us." I elbow him back.

"You're turning into quite the strategist," Simon smiles at me.

"Oh come on, guys, we're all the strategists. This bloody bathroom is like our very own war room."

They laugh; the mood is lighter thanks to our recent success.

"My biggest concern right now is Mateo. I'm worried what will happen to him and his family when we leave." I tuck my hands into my sleeves as I consider possible consequences.

"I'd say they should come, but a life on the run is no place for a young family." Luca says.

"I don't think there is a solution. If we leave a message to say we kept him out of our plans, they'll know we care enough to want to protect him and then he'll be in danger." Simon looks to each of us to confirm, and we all nod. There's no good solution for Mateo, aside from warning him before the event. It's the best we can do, but it doesn't make us feel any better about dragging him down with us.

"Are we nearly set on everything?" I look around at my team and feel, once again, the strength I gain from our camaraderie. We're a family, just like the rebels.

"I just need to get Shreya to give me a tour." Luca looks slightly embarrassed as he says this.

"Do what you have to. I'll write a note for you tonight." I should feel bad for Shreya being used but my jealousy won't quite allow it.

"When are we looking to do this?" Drummer asks.

"I was thinking, our next night shift rotation on Friday next week. What do you all think?" I reply.

"I think it sounds perfect. Close enough to make your balls shrink with fear, far enough away to feel fully prepared, but not too far that we lose momentum." Jono sums it up in in his usual style. He and Drummer look energised now we have a date. Great, they'll keep us up all day.

"I'll contact Ellyas now and tell him to prepare his raid for Thursday next week." Luca looks at his watch and gets up to retrieve the radio; he has a minute before he can make the call. The rest of us go back to the dorm.

I sit down cross-legged at the end of my bed and try to think what to write to my dad. I don't want the note to be traced back to us if it's found, or to get him in trouble. I close my eyes and think of him. On his desk he had a medallion in a glass box that his father had given to him on his eighteenth. I focus on the image.

It said *Quidvis Recte Factum Quamvis Humile Praeclarum — Whatever is rightly done, however humble, is noble.* It's the only Latin phrase I know. I'd read it so many times, and my dad had told me the meaning; sometimes he even quoted it to me. I draw the image and write out the Latin; he will know it's me. I make a capital 'Q' look like 'O' by floating a small squiggle underneath it, and then I capitalise an R – I – Q – T so the letters stand out, put the roman numerals for the date above the lion's head, and then 0300 under its head. It's not the subtlest code but I'm hoping that if the paper is found accidentally, and as it isn't expected, it won't be a clear message.

Luca nods to me when he comes back into the dorm; the message has been relayed. I hand him my note and then crawl under my covers and face away from Luca. I can't look at him knowing he's going to have to do "whatever it takes" to get inside the prison tomorrow. But, at least each of our sacrifices are small compared to some. It's nothing really. I keep telling myself that over and over again, but it doesn't help.

My night shift drags on and on; all I can think about is how Luca is getting Shreya to agree to him seeing the inside of the prison. I'm so stupid, harping on about a crush when the freedom of innocent people is at stake. But, I can't help it. By the time I return to the dorm that evening my stomach is in knots and I feel queasy. When Luca walks in he's looking bashful — Jono lets out a wolf whistle but is quickly silenced by Drummer, who gives him a meaningful look.

I can't avoid it; I need to know. "Well?"

"It's taken care of."

"Good, well done."

Luca grabs his towel and leaves the room. He doesn't even look at me.

I can't face the day or the others and so I climb into bed and try to sleep. The others must think I am sleeping because they begin whispering.

"What do you think he did to get in there?" Drummer asks Jono.

"Probably got in there, if you know what I mean," Jono sniggers.

"Everyone always knows what you mean, mate, you have the subtlety of a sheep."

"A sheep?"

"A sheep."

"Weird analogy."

"He seemed pretty embarrassed." Simon is chiming in now. I scowl, I thought at least he was above gossiping.

"Maybe, you know, he couldn't…" Jono must have mimed something.

They stop laughing when Luca enters and my body tenses as soon as I know he's in the room. Jono is the first to be brave enough to ask. "So?"

Luca hesitates. "So?"

"What happened?"

"Nothing." I can hear him getting into bed.

"You're not acting like nothing happened." Drummer's bed squeaks; he's probably leaning in to probe Luca further.

"It didn't, okay?" Jono and Drummer sigh in frustration but don't press Luca any further. I wish they had though; I'm burning to know what happened now.

By midday I'm still awake and I can hear Luca tossing and turning. I get up to leave, to be anywhere but near him, but he stirs.

"Cass?" His voice is heavy with tiredness.

"Mmmm."

"I just want you to know, that nothing happened. I mean that, nothing at all." He sounds sincere.

"Oh, well, why didn't you just tell the boys that?" I try to keep the pleasure from my voice but it's hard to disguise it.

"For her sake, I didn't want to embarrass her." He hugs his sheet close with one arm.

"Oh?"

"I just, I think I gave her the wrong impression." He looks down at the floor in shame.

"Oh. I see." I look down in shame too — there I am worrying about myself when I told Luca to flirt with her.

"I feel bad about leading her on. I think I hurt her."

I sit down on his bed next to him. "Look, we're all to blame on this one and I'm sorry that she got hurt, I really am."

He begins to rub his hand against my wrist. "I know." My pulse rate has quadrupled and I'm worried he'll feel it against the palm of his hand.

"Cass?" Luca looks up at me and begins to sit up, and I can feel a gentle tug against my arm.

"What time is it?" We've woken Simon up. I freeze, inches from Luca's face, and see the regret flood his eyes. I pull back.

"Just after midday, I think."

"I hate nights." He rolls over and pulls his sheet around himself. I look back at Luca who is lying down and he gives me a half smile.

"Couldn't sleep?" I shake my head and he pulls me down next to him and throws the sheet over us both. He curves his body around mine and kisses my neck once, lightly.

"Sweet dreams, Cassia."

I wake up hours later still cocooned in his arms. My neck is cricked and I'm boiling but I don't want to move, don't want the moment to end. Luca begins to stir and so I pretend to still be asleep. Despite the heat he nestles in closer, breathing me in. I don't know why but I hold my breath, terrified of breaking the moment. He brushes his lips oh so lightly against the back of my neck so that I break out in goose bumps. I curl further into his body, his hand running down the length of my thigh, and I begin to feel dizzy from continuing to hold my breath with anticipation. The sounds of the others shifting in their beds brings me back to reality abruptly. I move away a fraction and squeeze Luca's hand so that he'll understand. He buries his forehead in my hair and lets out a quiet but frustrated sigh. We lie there, holding hands, until the others are up. I can barely tear myself away but I need to get up and showered if I'm going to avoid clean-up duties.

We don't speak to one another over breakfast. Every time I look at him my throat constricts. All I can think about is being that close to him again; closer, even.

I can't work and the heat isn't helping with my muddled thoughts. *Focus Cassia,* I chant over and over. There is no way we're going to achieve a prison break when I'm so distracted. There's only one thing to get my brain back in the game; I need to get this feeling out of my system.

Tired, I make my way back to the dorm at the end of my shift. Luca is taking off his uniform when I walk in and I stop dead, my heart skipping a literal beat. He is having to peel off his top slowly because the heat has sealed it to his taut dark skin. I gulp, then collect myself — fortunately Drummer hasn't noticed my gawping. I walk over nonchalantly to my bed, and avoid looking at Luca at all.

"You lot coming down to play poker? Simon's already cleaning out Jono's stash of chocolate bars."

Chocolate bars, the gold of the army. Money doesn't get you far these days. Daytime poker is just a way of passing the time when your body clock is too screwed up to sleep — it's also in the mess hall, the old science lab, which has the closest thing to air con in the whole building, aside from the stinky gym.

"No thanks, I'm beat," I smile at Drummer.

"I might come down after a shower mate."

"Okay, see you there." He heads out, his back pocket bulging with sweets.

Luca looks at me briefly as if he wants to say something but is too embarrassed. He goes to leave but stops half way and turns. He only has his towel wrapped around his body.

Look at his *face* Cassia, I remind myself.

"I… ah…" He steps forward; I've never seen Luca look so uncomfortable.

"Is everything okay?"

He walks towards me and my pulse is pounding so vigorously through my entire body I'm sure he can see it.

"I just… if things were different here, I'd, I don't know… do all this differently, I guess." He opens out his arms to indicate us, but I'm too nervous to do anything but play the fool.

"All what?"

He steps closer. He's practically touching me now, so close I can feel the heat from his body. He cups my face in his hand and runs his thumb across my cheek. "Cass…" His voice is low and he leans in and kisses me. His kiss is soft and tender as he always is with me, but it's more than I can handle. I kiss him back, trying to control my longing for his touch, but he's withholding, almost teasing.

I step forward and press my body against his, needing more of him. Luca catches his breath as soon as our bodies touch and he pulls me closer, kisses me deeper, not like Luca at all. There's the creak of a floorboard outside the door as someone passes and we pull apart, out of breath. Luca looks deep into my eyes with loaded meaning. He picks up my towel and leads me by the hand into the shower room, the only room with a lock.

Luca locks the door and turns on the shower. He hangs up our towels and stands before me in just his boxers. I am feeling awkward and unsure of myself now that the moment is broken. He comes towards me again and looks at me with all the longing we've both been suppressing. He pulls me to him and picks me up around my waist and carries me under the shower. I want to laugh but I don't want us to get caught; instead, I tilt my head back and let the water cool my burning body. Luc smiles up at me and then, catching sight of my now see-through tank top, he runs his hand slowly, maddeningly, down the side of my torso.

He lifts my top over my head and lets it fall, heavy, to the floor. He kisses me deeply, achingly, and slowly undoes my trousers and lets them join my discarded top.

Before this moment I've only ever kissed guys, nothing more, but I'm not thinking about that. All I can think about is drowning myself in him.

I'm not thinking.

I want all of him but luckily one of us is being smart. "No, Cass, we can't."

I feel stung by his rebuff but he explains shyly. "We don't have anything…" Of course, how can I have been so reckless?

"Oh, right, yeah." I hope the steam-filled cubicle hides my embarrassment.

"Believe me, there's nothing I want more." He smiles at me and kisses me, more languidly this time.

"You're not helping the situation, you know."

"Cassia, stop talking."

I raise an eyebrow at him, and allow myself to get lost in the moment all over again. After our shower we manage to sleep all day in my tiny little bed.

Luckily, when night falls the others don't seem suspicious of Luc and I sharing a bed as it's something we've done so many times before. When we wake up, Luca hangs back tying his boot laces as everyone else goes down for food, and then pulls me to him and kisses me.

"I need to shower with you again, like now."

I laugh and push him away. "If we're late we'll be on cleaning duty and it'll be the last thing we'll want to do."

He picks me up and squeezes me. "I can't take it!"

"Maybe later."

"Yes, later." He puts me down and kisses me again, and I have to pull away. "Who is on with you tonight?"

"Harold."

Luca grins at that.

"Why?"

"No reason."

No reason turns out to be a 3am visit and an explicit show-and-tell in the not-very-pleasant bathroom.

As Luca is leaving he says, "I thought wanting you before was bad, but I think this is worse."

"I know what you mean."

"All I can think about is you. Even now I want you more than I did before."

"Can we just lock ourselves away for a week to get it out of our systems?"

Luca feigns shock. "A week? More like six months."

"Or a year."

"Say that again."

"A year?" I ask, perplexed.

He leans in and kisses me, locking the door behind him. "It's the way you say it," he whispers into my ear, "and the images it conjures."

When Luca finally leaves I peer around the corner of the office, terrified Harold has heard everything that has just happened, but fortunately the man can sleep through absolutely everything. Glowing and content, I sit back at my desk and dream of the day when we finally get out of Camburg and Luca and I can truly be alone.

On Friday I have my day off and I go to see mum on her lunch break. I'm willing myself to stay awake so that I can sleep through the night. Mum is taking tablets when I enter; I feel guilty when I notice, I haven't been thinking about her health enough.

"How are you doing being back at work?"

"I'm fine." She knows I'm not buying it. "Okay, a little tired but generally fine."

"When's your next test?"

"It was last week, results Monday."

"Mum, I'm so sorry I didn't know, I've been so selfish."

"Don't be silly, you've been incredible. Now, tell me what's going on with you, you seem… different." She looks at me coyly.

"You should have been a detective. Fine, as I forgot to make sure you were doing well… Luca and I are… well…" Huh, I don't know what to call it. *Fooling around* — urgh, that sounds horrible. *Dating* — hardly, we can't exactly "date".

"Seeing each other?"

"Yes. Seeing each other."

Mum beams. "Good, I always liked him, such a good young man."

"Mmmm hmmm."

"So…?"

"So, what?"

"How's it going, you know…"

"Mum, no, we're not going to talk about *that* and no, we haven't." Sometimes Mum can be horrifyingly nosey.

"I just want you to…"

"Stop. Just stop right there. No, we are not talking about this. We haven't. I am still, you know, so let's leave it at that and *never* speak of this again." Mum just laughs and hugs me. The mortification.

On my way out, Mum takes a patient into her office. I sneak into the supply closet and smuggle out a handful of contraband... Well, I want to be prepared.

After seeing mum I'm desperate to find Luca. I want to go down to the lake with him so we don't have to worry about anyone finding us. After an exhaustive search I give up and go to Mateo's house, guilt niggling at me that I should warn him about our plans and how they might affect him.

Milena opens the door to me; Mateo is playing with the children in their box-sized lounge. The warmth and love in their tiny home make me feel all the more ashamed for what I am going to bring to their home. They just want to keep their children safe and I'm taking that away. Seeing his family is exactly what I need, a wakeup call. I'm using Luca as an escape; there's far too much at stake for me to lose sight of what we want to achieve.

Before I leave Mateo's I take him to one side. "Things are going to get bad next week. We're worried you're going to be implicated. Find a way to protect yourself, to disassociate yourself from us."

"It's okay, you no have worry."

"I am worried. They'll question you. I don't know what the best thing is for your family; a life on the run is definitely not the answer."

Mateo holds my hand firmly. "You must fight, I must look after family. We both do what is right." He grins at me with such warmth that I think my heart might crumble. "We be okay."

I hug Mateo tight and leave without being able to look at his family. If anything happens to them, it will be on me and I won't be able to live with myself.

Inside the dining hall I finally find Luca and he immediately knows something is wrong.

"I saw Mateo."

I don't need to say anything more; he's feeling it too. Our fun is over. Everything is about to change.

WEEK TWELVE

On Monday evening we all sit around idly as Luca uses the radio to contact Ellyas.

"We've made contact with some other groups. The message is spreading — Friday is the day when we start to take back what is ours, over." Ellyas sounds both happy and sad.

"And you've got the coordinates I gave you for our rendezvous, over?" Luca asks.

"Yeah, we'll see you there at first light on Saturday, over." I listen for optimism but I only hear anxiety. Something is niggling at me so I speak up.

"Will all of you be there, over?" I ask.

Ellyas hesitates and static bubbles up to fill the beat before he confirms that they will be. His hesitation tells me all I need to know. Jake is up to something.

Later that night I climb into bed with Luca. "Jake is going to do something reckless. I just know he is."

Luca lets out a weary sigh. "I was thinking the same thing."

"What can we do?"

"I don't know. I don't know how you can stop someone who is so filled with hate."

I bury my face in Luca's neck. "Sometimes I wish we hadn't gone down this path, that we'd just accepted our fate."

"Never accept your fate, never stop fighting. Okay?"

I breathe in deeply, remembering him, remembering this moment of calm, of comfort. I'll need it one day. "Okay."

Thursday comes too quickly. The air is weighted with humidity; it sits unforgivingly in our lungs and clings to our clothes and skin with poisonous intent. What's worse is that Kohler has returned.

At dinner, Major Burgin sits with Naples and Greek and some other soldiers I don't know by name but recognise. I sit with Simon, and we eat in nervous silence.

"Is it a bad sign?" Simon whispers.

"As in from up high? Fate telling us to not go ahead?" I twirl my spaghetti around my fork.

"Yeah."

"At this point, most things are going to tell us not to go ahead. And yes, it is a bad sign in a non-theological way too."

"Oh?"

"We'll talk about it later."

"Okay." Simon is pushing his food around and not eating.

"You okay?"

"Just anxious." He puts his fork down, giving up on the suspicious-looking stew in front of him.

I give him a reassuring smile. "No one's forcing you to do this with us. And no one is going to make you eat whatever that is."

His lips twitch into a smile. "I don't need to be forced, it's just, I feel like we're taking on Goliath."

"David won though."

"It's just a story."

"We've taken our time; we've planned for every eventuality we can think of, we just have to believe that we're taking them by surprise and that our strategy will pay off." I lean forward. "If we don't believe that then we may as well resign ourselves to be their prisoners for the rest of our lives."

Simon nods, almost convinced. I just hope that I've given the impression that I actually believe what I just said because honestly, I'm starting to think we're just a bunch of stupid kids.

That evening we sit around again with the radio centre stage. We switch it on every fifteen minutes, waiting for the first signal from Ellyas. At 12:15am it comes.

Static hisses through the line. "Sault, over?" Fortunately he's remembered to use the call signs we designated. Sault is the call sign for our group.

"Are you there yet, over?"

The line jumps and crackles.

"We've contained the perimeter, we're going in. We'll be in touch, out." The line goes dead. We all sit in silence; my pulse filling my ears with its thrumming. The minutes are painful; not even Jono or Drummer are able to think of something to say.

Fifteen minutes pass and nothing.

Thirty. Still nothing.

Forty-five minutes and the static on the radio dances. "We're out and on our way to our safe house. Pack heading to the drop zone now, over." Pack is the call sign for Jake's group.

"Thank you, stay safe, over."

"You too. Out."

We remain in silence a little longer, collectively relieved but anxious that our turn is to come.

"We should get some sleep." Luca stands and holds out his hand to help me up. In our room I don't care about what the others think; Luca and I get into bed together once again and lie awake, in silence, for most of the night.

Luca and I go for a run the next morning wearing our backpacks as we're the only ones who regularly go out of bounds and so, hopefully, it won't raise suspicion. We cut back round the perimeter of Camburg, keeping to the trees, and check out the drop site. Sure enough there are three backpacks with electroshock weapons (or ES guns) and a few other goodies they've collected in their midnight raid. I remove one weapon and a few other items as I won't be able to meet with everyone until I've taken down the security systems. Luca takes a few pieces himself, the rest will be collected at night, before the prison break. We cover over the bags again and run back to the lake.

The water is still, opening up another world the exact mirror of ours below its surface. I wonder what another world like ours, but without the GDO, would be like. I skim a stone across the surface and watch as the ripples burst the perfect picture on the surface. How easy it is to destroy, but then the water calms and everything is back to how it was. If only it was always that simple.

Luca is sitting on the bank looking out across the water when I go to join him.

"Something doesn't feel right."

"How do you mean?"

"This plan, it's too… easy."

"Not everything has to be hard, Cass."

I inhale deeply. I put my hand in Luca's for comfort. "I'm terrified that we're being reckless, that we're setting everyone up for a fall."

"But we can't just let everything that's been happening keep on happening, like Lillian." Luca speaks softly but I shudder, despite the heat. I hope that Ellyas will be able to recover from what the GDO did to her.

"What about the repercussions? And there will be ones, big ones." My hands begin to shake. Whenever I have the chance, I've been accessing the GDO mainframe looking at their files. There are videos, hundreds of them, that show executions, the piling up of bodies on the streets. Torture. Men, women and children, they slaughter whomever they feel stands in their way. The woman holding her baby in Camburg flashes into my mind. What kind of hell will they unleash in retaliation? What harm will come to innocent people because of us, because of me? The shaking gets worse.

"Cassia…? Cass, it's okay, it's going to be okay." Luca holds me tight, trying to fight off my fears for me.

"If you'd seen…"

"I know, I know. But we have to free your dad; we have to give other rebels the opportunity to fight back. We're only responsible for what happens here." I cling to him with desperation, knowing what's to come, whether we succeed or not. People will die because of a computer virus that I'm going to plant. I don't know if I can live with that.

"I was going to wait until your eighteenth, but I want to give you something now." Luca pulls a gold necklace out of his pocket. The small pendant catches the sunlight and it blinks back at me; it's a lotus flower.

"Luc, it's beautiful."

He fastens it around my neck. "It was my mum's; it's one of the few things she managed to bring with her from Africa."

"I can't take it if it's precious to her."

Luca smiles at me warmly. "She *wanted* you to have it." I touch the cool gold pendant at my neck. "She told me what it means; she felt it would give you strength."

"What does it mean?"

"The lotus flower grows in ponds and has to fight its way through murky water to get to the sun. When it finally breaks through the darkness it blooms."

"So, I guess that makes me stuck in the mud at the moment."

Luca smiles and gives me a soft kiss. "But you will make it through, because you're strong."

"Okay, enough metaphors. I love it." My throat burns with emotion and so I pull Luca into a tight embrace.

We talk for as long as we feel we can before we have to get back to Camburg. My nerves are getting the better of me and before we run out and away from the cover of the trees, Luca stops me and holds me firmly against the nearest tree. His kiss is sorrowful; it feels like a goodbye. I can't breathe from the weight of it and so I pull away and look into his worried eyes.

"I will do anything for you, Cass; I need you to know that."

"Me too." I pull him close to me again, feeling the weight and life of him against me. "Please be safe. I couldn't... I just couldn't cope if something were to happen to you."

"I will. You too, Cass, you too."

Breaking away from him feels impossible but we both know that we have to get back, have to appear normal. Raising suspicion could mean the end of us all.

We wave to the guards as we run into Camburg and stop to stretch outside our base, something we usually do. We walk slowly back inside, trying to come up with inane topics of conversation, but we keep going back to commenting on the heat. Inside the dorm we let out a guilty laugh; we're terrible at acting normal.

I trudge through the rest of the day; it feels endless. It's only when my night shift begins that time seems to escape me and all of a sudden it's 11pm. Jaidee is asleep on the sofa; I've had to drug him. My mum will meet Luca at the main gates where he'll let her out as soon as the security system goes down. She'll meet everyone at the hatch and we'll all head to our rendezvous point with Ellyas, Yve, Jake, and the others.

The guards in the prison rotate at midnight, and that will be my cue. I double, triple, quadruple check I have the viruses. I do dummy runs of executing the plan. I keep checking the monitors, making sure everyone is in position, that everyone is okay. I find it hard to take my attention away from the screen with Luca on it.

11:55. I put the USB drives into the computer. I turn up the heat in the server room.

11:56. I check Jaidee is still deep asleep. I check my perimeter.

11:57. I steady my palms. Take a sip of water.

11:58. I check on the others; they're all looking anxious.

11:59. I hold my breath and prepare the files.

12:00. Kohler walks into the room.

"Fortis." I can't help but jump.
"Sir?"
"Why haven't you woken up Jaidee?"
I am positive he can see that something is up, I'm sure of it. My chest hurts my heart is beating so fast.
"I can cope on my own."

He sneers; there's something in his eyes that frightens me.

"I need you in my office." He turns and marches out of the room. I have no choice but to go ahead. I activate the viruses and eject the drives, slipping them into my pocket, and make my way to his office.

As I leave the room the computers begin to freeze and shut down around me. I ignore them. The CCTV screens turn to black and I just keep on walking. I need to buy us time; I need Kohler not to notice. I need to distract him.

When I walk into his office, Kohler's eyes are on my chest. It's only then that I realise I've undone three buttons in my uniform. I hesitate but don't do them up. What's the point? But his ogling makes me uneasy. He seems less in control than usual. He takes a swig from a mug on his desk, and that's when I twig that he's drunk.

He comes around his desk and stands too close, his hot sweet breath seeping over me.

I try to keep my head. "What can I do for you, sir?"

He laughs and there's a flash of a hyena. "Always such a tease, Fortis. With your little meek 'what can I do for you, sir?'"

He steps closer so that he's almost touching me, his face millimetres from mine. "You know exactly what you can do for me, you little slut. Look at you with your shirt unbuttoned, slick with sweat like a showgirl. Putting it all on display for me, aren't you?"

I step back, not wanting to anger him, afraid of making the situation worse than it already was. "Not at all sir, it's a hot night, I didn't know you'd be here."

"Do you think about me, Fortis? Do you think about me overpowering you?"

"No, sir."

"I bet you do, in your little bed at night, you think about me and I bet it makes you shudder with pleasure, you little whore."

"No, sir," I've backed away to the door; I'm close, so close, to freedom.

"I bet you service all those men who share a room with you. Keep them all at your whim. Especially the black one. He's your favourite isn't he?"

I don't answer. The doorframe is behind me now; I could make a break for it.

"Like in the shower room, you like to take him in the shower room, don't you?"

Suddenly it doesn't seem like he's guessing. "And in the toilets, and where was it the other day? Oh yes, in the gym supply closet. But you've been saving yourself for me, haven't you Fortis?"

"I don't know what you're talking about."

"I told you I'd be watching you, and I have, and your little rebellion with your little friends. What a stupid slut you are, and I thought you were supposed to be smart." He sways very slightly and runs his hand through his damp hair.

My left hand finds the doorknob behind my back.

"And whilst you're in here with me, your little plan is falling apart."

"I don't know what you mean." But I have to know how much he's found out before I can leave, and I really want to leave.

I look at the camera and he dismisses it. "Disabled, thanks to you, remember?"

He knows everything then.

"What plan?"

"The prison break tonight, the coordinated attacks. Your little virus. You led us straight to the rebels who have been plaguing us." Panic floods my veins.

"A virus?" I try and keep my voice steady.

"Well, you see, the virus I kept to myself. No harm in all the cameras being down tonight, so we can deal with you all as we wish." He smiles to himself and I start to feel some relief.

"Did you know there were two viruses?"

He pauses, suddenly wary.

"One that shuts down the cameras here instantly and one that burrows its way into SINN and disables and destroys *everything*. The GDO will be left blind and broken. How are you going to find the plague without any eyes?"

He lunges at me, panicked, and I spin round, flinging the door open to run but he's anticipated my move. He grabs me by the arm and pulls me back close to his body. He's aroused and I begin to panic. He's stronger than me and he's been drinking; there's no way I can reason with him.

He licks my neck slowly.

My body is frozen with fear. I can't scream. Why can't I scream?

Shock. I'm in shock.

"Good thing that when I'm done with you, no one will know that I withheld that information."

He pushes me so hard against the wall that my head cracks against it. I blink away the momentary blackness and then he's ripping and tearing at my clothes. I am watching as if from a distance but I force myself to return to my own body and I begin to fight him, lashing out and scratching him across his face, drawing blood. All my training with Mateo is paying off. His rage increases and he pulls at my hair so I kick him in the groin. He gasps, but immediately retaliates with a right hook to my jaw. I stumble to the side. He grabs the front of my shirt and pulls down, ripping it open.

"Bitch." He grabs me squarely by the shoulders and I headbutt him. My ears ring, but it forces him off me. I run out of the office and make it to the hall. He catches part of my shirt and I trip, falling hard onto my wrist. I let out a scream of pain. I'm on my front and he begins tugging at my trousers.

"No!" I scream — my voice is hoarse and strained. He's busy fumbling with himself and so my arms are free. Howling, I use my arms to push up from the floor. My wrist feels like it's snapped under the exertion. Kohler topples and I kick out at him, right in the knee cap. He yells and curses. I turn and try to haul myself up, Kohler grapples at my legs, trying to pull me down. I knee him in the face and scrabble for the stairs. He's right behind me, panting, raging.

My bag is at the bottom of the stairs. I lunge for it and rip open the front pocket; I take out what's inside and roll onto my back, and Kohler's eyes flash in fear as I pull the trigger. There's a crack and a jolt as 50,000 volts embed themselves into his right shoulder. He collapses to the floor and jolts before he passes out. Trembling, I grab my bag and only look back once to see he's pissed himself.

I don't have time to think, I just run for the prison. I'm late and everything we planned has fallen apart. My wrist jars with every step but I keep on, trying to shake off the feeling of dizziness that is setting in. The only thing that can save me now is getting out of Camburg and away from the GDO. I'll never survive the GDO after all that has happened; I have to get out.

I pause in the shadows outside the prison and take stock of the situation. I can't see the patrol guards, and squinting it looks like the gate is unlocked. Running on adrenalin alone I bolt for the outer entrance and slip inside. Keeping myself as hidden as possible, I make my way to the main entrance. The earth is dry beneath my feet and dust billows around me, cloaking my movements. The heavy, reinforced metal door is also ajar — I push it gently and make my way inside. It doesn't make sense. If the GDO knows our plan, why is the prison broken into? I shut the door behind me and the lock clicks in place. I was always going to be the last in, and it's my job to secure the front. I turn to the keypad and, taking a hammer out of my backpack, and left-handed, I smash it to pieces — no need for fancy re-wiring here. I walk down the dimly lit hall — only the emergency lighting is working; the backup generator is still on. Going through SINN I'd managed to find an override code to the door locks for when the prison is on emergency power — Drummer and Jono must have managed the hack I gave them. Well done, boys. The second door is also open for me, and I deal with the lock the same way as I have before. I am becoming quite attached to my hammer.

I am finally at the main desk where prisoners are checked in — and slumped on the floor, handcuffed to a railing, are two unconscious guards who are drooling slightly. I wonder how long the shock will keep them down. I feel a twinge of guilt but at least they aren't seriously hurt. As I approach the door leading to the inside of the prison, the commotion inside starts to become obvious. I take my knife from my pack and secure it in my belt. I pick up my pace, gently cradling my right hand to try and prevent the vibrations in my wrist causing me to feel any fainter.

Finally, after some weaving through hallways, I come out into the central courtyard where there's a sea of guards who must have been waiting in ambush but they are still outnumbered by prisoners, who are fighting harder than they would have expected of bureaucrats. Most of the prisoners are constrained; only a few are still fighting. Simon is standing with the guards. Drummer is handcuffed with a plastic tie. I stay back in the shadows and kneel behind a pillar at one of the four entrances into the courtyard. I swing my bag off my back and slowly unzip the main compartment to reveal the backup plan.

Carefully, I take out three canisters and peer into the melee. Watching the chaos, I wait for an opportunity, I arm the three weapons and place one next to the pillar where I am crouching. The other two I roll out into the courtyard in different directions aiming for two of the other exits, but I make sure to leave our escape route clear.

I wait; I need to get Luca or Jono's attention before taking things further. Eventually, I catch Jono's eye. I nod to him and he begins to fall back to the exit. Luca spots the movement and begins to do the same. I notice my father for the first time and my breath catches; he must have been briefed by the others because he begins to drag other prisoners towards the exit. The fight is still raging among the final few who haven't been detained. Separate from the fighting is a cluster of GDO soldiers guarding the prisoners they've re-captured; they're my main target. Luca has circled back and is at the entrance opposite to mine. He nods. It's time. I arm the canister in my hand and he does the same, and we throw them into the group of soldiers. As they land I compress the remote trigger and then start the timer on my watch. Gas hisses violently from the metal flasks causing the ones I threw to spin in circles. Luca, Jono and I put on our masks. The soldiers begin to choke as Luca and I launch ourselves at the ones holding prisoners.

I shock one soldier with my ES gun and whip the butt of it across the temple of another. I try to use my weapon again but it won't fire, so I ram my heel down into the instep of the soldier next to me. Taking out my knife, I cut through the cable ties holding the two women kneeling on the floor —I haul them to their feet, indicate for them to cover their mouths, stay low and run to the exit I'm pointing out, which is where Jono is standing, waiting. Luca has freed Drummer who now has his mask on and is helping with the evacuation.

I spot Simon who has managed to get his mask on as well and run to him and press the 'com link on my mask. The GDO really do have some good toys.

"Start heading out."

"No, Cassia."

"What?" I look at my watch unable to focus on what Simon's just said; a minute has passed. Some of the guards are now stumbling around.

Then I remember; Simon was standing with the soldiers when I first arrived. I look at him, "Why?"

"Look around you Cassia, it's exactly how it was before. It will never end unless we just stop. The fighting needs to stop."

"No, you're just giving up."

"He told them about us." Jono is behind me when I turn, bruised and bloody.

"They already knew though." Simon looks saddened but not ashamed of his choice. Rage boils inside me and with my left hand I rip his mask from his face. I am about to punch him when a hand grabs my wrist. Simon begins desperately to put his mask back on.

"We need to get out of here." It's Luca. I look around and almost all the prisoners are out of the courtyard. Drummer is leading the final few out, who are struggling under the effects of the gas.

"He knows where we're going. He'll have told them."

"Remember our backup plan?" I hadn't had time to tell Simon that we'd thought of a secondary option for our escape whilst we were at the lake. After Luca and I had decided last minute on a alternative for the prison break we felt it was also important to have another option for the escape destination too.

"Won't he still be able to lead them there?"

"We take him with us." Luca pulls Simon's arms behind his back and whips out a cable tie. Simon begins yelling in protest but Luca pushes him towards Jono who takes him to our planned exit.

I turn and survey the slowly dissipating scene and catch sight of Shreya struggling with a prisoner. I run over and pull her off him and push him towards Drummer. She looks at me, her face red with indignation.

"How *could* you?" She sways slightly. I put Simon's mask on her and 'com her.

"I'm sorry, we had to."

"Why didn't you tell me?" She looks so hurt and I feel awful.

"We didn't want to implicate any more people than we had to. It's a dangerous plan." Also, I didn't know if she could be trusted, but I don't think saying that will help matters.

"I'm coming with you."

"I can't guarantee your safety."

"I don't need you to do anything for me except to keep your ES gun in your belt." I don't bother telling her it's jammed. It's a good speech from her. No point in making our relationship any frostier.

"Okay." I really hope I'm not going to regret this decision. I swing her arm around my neck and help her towards the final few escapees, her feet dragging slightly as my watch alarm beeps merrily. Shreya sags; the mask came too late.

"Shit…" I try to hold her up but she's taller than me. I feel my knees begin to go when I spot Luca. He comes over and easily lifts her into his arms.

"I'll take her outside, you help the others affected."

I help the stumbling stragglers to the tunnel door where there's a rising sense of panic, hopefully we got the prisoners away from the smoke quickly enough. Their noise level is steadily increasing. Not knowing what else to do, I pull my mask up onto my head so I can speak.

"Quickly, quietly." I sound like a hall monitor. I'm terrified they'll raise suspicion by being too noisy when they reach the forest.

Finally, I see my dad a few feet ahead. I run to him and he holds me like I'm made of spun sugar. I pull away reluctantly.

"Dad, you have to go through."

"Not without you."

I smile. "I've got this. You need to go, and you need to tell them all that they *have* to be quiet. We can't alert the other guards to where we're escaping to."

"The virus worked then?" Drummer asks. I turn to see he's also risked removing his mask.

"Lights out, cameras out; let's just hope the other one is doing just as well."

"What other one?" Dad looks at us, no idea what's going on.

"Dad, will you just go already? Jeez."

He lets out a low chuckle of surprise and salutes me as he follows the others.

The soldiers in the prison are all unconscious when Jono goes back and does a final sweep; they'll be out for at least two hours. Last, Drummer and I make our way to the tunnel. I haven't seen Luca for a while. I hope he's okay but I have to focus on the final job — sealing the passageway. We close the door and begin hammering planks of wood across the frame. I'm pretty hopeless with my one hand, even though I've been relatively efficient wielding a hammer left-handed. Another hand gently takes the hammer from me. I spin around alert for danger, and see Luca.

"Need some help?" He looks at me with deep concern; he can see something more than a fight has happened. I try to stop my eyes from betraying me. Now isn't the time. Too many people need us.

"I'm okay but my wrist is screwed." He takes over without a word, his body tense. There's an unspoken understanding. Later.

"Do you think Ellyas took our advice?"

"Yeah, he said it was the smart thing to do."

All three of us head quickly up the tunnel. We re-seal it at the top and cover it over with leaves and moss, brushing away footprints as we go. It will be easy for them to track us with so many people leaving a trail but we have to delay them as much as we can. We then run for the trees, exhaustion already pounding inside my bones.

When we finally reach the lake my breathing is laboured, I'm struggling more than I thought I would. Luca keeps looking at me, worried. At the shore my mum and dad are waiting, still clutching onto each other, terrified that if they let go they'll lose one another again. My mum lets out a gasp of mixed relief and horror at my appearance.

"What happened?"

"I think I broke my wrist." I hold it out to her feeling like a wounded puppy.

"I brought medical supplies."

"Thanks. We don't have time though, we have to keep moving. Did you get out okay?"

"Yes, there were less guards about." That's because most of them were at the prison, waiting for us.

She rustles around in her bag and hands me two pills. "For the pain." I knock them back and turn to see Drummer and Luca covering the tracks around the lake. My mum nods and steps into the water, leading my dad. He takes her bag from her and they walk into the inky depths. Luca, Drummer, and I stand with our feet in the water and, using our canteens, we slosh water up onto the shore, trying to eradicate all evidence of footprints. Satisfied, we wade further into the lake. Originally we planned to head west, finding our way to near where the work fields are so we could cross the border but instead, we turn north, to cross the lake and then, once across, we'll carry on north, towards the mountains.

We walk along, waist deep and in silence. The air out here is so clear that the stars and moon light our way. Occasionally I feel a curious fish brush against my leg and I almost want to smile at the innocence of it. The lake stretches for miles around but our way across is roughly one mile. My right wrist is throbbing and painful despite the painkillers, but I try to ignore it and keep moving. Soon the water deepens and I tentatively lower my pack into the water. I'm not convinced that these packs really are totally waterproof and that they float. To my relief my pack bobs in front of me. I lean on it gratefully and use it as a swimming aid as I make my way across the water.

The surface is so calm around us that it's like swimming through a rippling dream, smooth and hypnotic. When we're about three quarters of the way across the sounds of the search party begin to dance through the night air. I look behind me and can make out the faint glimmer of torches among the trees. My heart rate picks up and the three of us share a look of mutual fear. We knew this would happen though, and we've been really lucky that they've only just managed to get a team out here. We press on, my only comfort being that I can barely make out the shapes of my parents who are not too far ahead, let alone the hundred and fifty or so prisoners. I just hope the prisoners are managing to swim despite the gas they inhaled.

When we decided we needed a new location to head to, Luca remembered he'd heard from Ellyas of a town near the border that was filled with Resistance sympathisers — being close to allies was important. And fresh water. Near the town was a village called Vayo in the valley of a range of mountains. At the base was forest, in the mountains trees and a fresh waterfall, and nearby the town was filled with food and people who could help. It's a good option, just so long as the

GDO doesn't find us. We just have to hope that they won't be able to mobilise properly without their communications system up and running.

At last we reach the bank where we are going to make our way through the forest. The group are waiting for us.

"Everything okay?" I whisper to Jono.

"Some are still a bit groggy but fresh air and a freezing lake seem to be helping." He chuckles, "the poor sods".

"Let's get moving; the search party has started up." He nods and the group begins to move. Jono is in front with the map, with Drummer on lookout. Luca and I stay at the back with my parents. We don't dare talk or rest. Our unit walks through the deep dark shadows of the trees in eerie silence and finally, after an hour we reach the base of the mountain range. This is where we'll meet the others but they aren't here yet. There's a few more hours trekking to go, and we've made good time, but it's important that everyone stops to drink. We take it in turns to drink from the fresh stream of water coming down from the mountain; another benefit of our new location.

A lot of the group are still a little woozy from the gas but most of them now seem revived. Shreya is helped to sit by two prisoners. Simon is sitting sullenly by himself, his arms resecured behind his back after the lake crossing. As content as I can be with how everyone is doing, I go and sit down with my mum.

My mum straps up my wrist, as gently as possible, but I still felt sick with pain every time she touches it.

"I can't feel a break but that's not to say there isn't one. More likely a fracture, which is good because it won't need re-setting, just healing." She hands me a bottle of ibuprofen.

"Every four hours for the pain and swelling."

"Thanks, Mum."

She looks at me intently, her face filled with wonder. "You are so brave, we are so proud of you."

I swallow back my tears. I can't break now, we're not there yet. "Life is just going to get harder, you know that right? We'll forever be watching our backs."

"It's better than living in a cage." I turn to see my dad; he's brought my mum a flask filled with water, which she takes gratefully.

"Mum, you doing okay? If you need rest, we can stay longer."

"Never better." She looks at my dad in that infinite way that people who love each other so deeply do.

"And you, Cassia? What really happened?" I turn away.

"Oh, you know —" I can feel my voice catching. I swallow hard. "Just got into a scrap with a guard, no biggy."

My parents exchange a look.

"Later, we'll talk about this later." I smile a shaky smile as I go to find Luca, relieved to be able to bury my feelings again.

"Anything?" Luca shakes his head. The radio is in his hand.

I look out into the forest but can't see any movement.

"What time is it?"

"02:11." I put my hand reassuringly on his arm.

"They'll be here."

The radio begins to crackle with static; we both watch it expectantly.

"Sault? Sault? Over."

"Pack? You okay? Over."

"We —" The radio bursts into static again. "We're on our way, had to ditch the car, an hour behind schedule but we're in the trees, under cover. Over."

"Did you get the packages okay? Over."

"Yeah, they're with me. Over." Luca lets out a sigh of relief, his parents are safe.

"Thank God. We'll wait. Over."

"No, keep going. Get the payload to safety. Over."

"You sure? Over."

"Yeah —" There's something in Ellyas' voice that halts my feeling of relief. "Viper went back. Over." Viper is Jake's call sign.

You know when you've gone out and you can't shake that niggling feeling that something's not right and you get home and you left the iron on or something? Well, I've had that same feeling all evening and with that, *Viper went back*, I know what it is. I'd seen it in his eyes. Jake was never really going to listen to me; he liked our plan, sure. It was the perfect distraction for what he needs to achieve — to blow up GDO headquarters.

I grab the radio off Luc. "Is he alone? Over."

I can hear the hesitation and reluctance in Ellyas' voice over the static. "No, Cobra went with him. Over." Meaning Yve.

If my parents hadn't been within hearing distance, I probably would have sworn more but because of their presence I confine myself to a few choice expletives.

Luca says goodbye to Ellyas and turns to me. "Now what?"

"I knew it was too good to be true, I knew that Jake wasn't really with us." I begin to pace and a couple of people watch me with alarm — clearly worried that our pursuers are pretty close if one of the teen soldiers is freaking out.

"I have to go after him. I have to stop him."

Luca looks at me sorrowfully. "No, you don't."

"Yes Luc, yes, I do."

"You can't save him from himself."

"I have to try."

"Cassia, no."

I look into his dark eyes. "Luca, don't tell me what I can't do. I can't just let him do this. What if he kills innocent people? Doing this... doing this is going to change him forever. He will never come back from this."

"It's too reckless, the GDO knows that rebels are out on the streets tonight — you won't get away a second time."

"It doesn't matter, I have to try and stop him."

"You know, it's one of the things that I —" He pauses, as if he's holding himself back. "— really admire about you, that you will do anything for the people you love. Even if it means you make impulsive decisions."

"Wouldn't you?"

He looks at me so intensely I feel my stomach flutter with emotion. "I would." Then he tells Jono he's going back to Amphora with me to get Jake.

"No, Luc, you don't have to," I protest. I don't want to drag him into another one of my rash choices.

He looks at me and kisses me lightly. "Anything."

Trying to convince my parents that I have to leave is a little harder.

"No, absolutely not." Dad glares at Luc as if he's the one leading me astray.

"Dad, I'm going, it's Jake. I have to." Luca stays silent, not wanting to make things worse.

"Look, I'm a soldier now and I'm pretty much eighteen, you can't stop me."

"We're your parents. If I had known you were planning this, I would never have agreed to it."

"Well, you did."

"I didn't know you were the one orchestrating it! I thought you were just asked to pass a note that only I would understand!" My dad looks incredulous.

I'm not proud of this but it's kind of a classic teen move. "Mum didn't have a problem with me joining the GDO and springing you from prison."

Whilst my parents fight I sneak away; pretty shitty of me seeing as they've just been reunited, but I have to save Jake.

We leave one of our backpacks with the group and take the other one between us with our water bottles filled. It will be an hour before we reach the nearest town where hopefully we can steal a car so we can get to Amphora before Jake makes the biggest mistake of his life.

We walk quickly but don't run; there's no point in tiring ourselves out and the jolting would put my wrist in agony. When we're about a mile from our group I can feel Luca become agitated, and I immediately tense. Has he sensed something?

"What is it?" I whisper, looking around, but I can't see anyone.

"Nothing, I don't hear anything. Do you?"

"No, I thought you had?" He glances at me quizzically.

"You seem tense."

"Oh, yeah…"

"What's going on? Is it Jake?"

Luca looks away from me as we keep walking, his hands locked into fists.

"I don't want to push you but, was it Kohler?"

My breath catches and I can't remember how my usual breathing sounds. I don't want to give away my panic but I can't remember the damned rhythm. I'm concentrating on getting it back when I realise Luca has stopped. The expression on his face is so pained that it makes my insides crumble. I'm not strong enough to deal with his pain on top of my own. I can't. I need him to be strong right now.

"We have to get to Jake." The sadness on his face is like daggers; I turn from him and start walking again as treacherous tears spring from my eyes. My skin is still crawling from Kohler's touch; I can still smell his sickly sweet breath and feel the weight of him on top of me. But he didn't defeat me; I hadn't let him. I'd fought back. Luca should know that Kohler didn't get to have me, that I stopped him, but I can't say the words. They are lodged in my throat, suffocating me. I'm being ridiculous — nothing happened! Why am I even upset?

Luca's hand rests gently on my shoulder and I instinctively flinch. He pulls his hand away quickly, as if he's harmed me in some way.

"I'm sorry, Cass. I'm so sorry." His voice catches and we stand with him behind me, silent in the middle of the forest.

"He didn't, you know…" I manage to say, and I hear a shuddering breath behind me. I turn and Luca is knelt on the floor, his face in his hands.

"I should have protected you. I should have been there." He begins to rip up roots from around him. I kneel down opposite him.

"We didn't know he'd be there."

He looks at me, his eyes pools of misery.

"It's not your job to be my protector Luc, ever since my dad was taken you've been there for me, but you can't hold yourself responsible for my safety."

"Yes I can." He reaches out, then pulls back apologetically. I inch forward and pick up his hand and gently hold it. I let out a shuddering breath.

"I'm so sorry, Cassia. I'm so sorry."

"I'm okay," I lie.

"No, you're not, but I'm going to do whatever it takes, whatever you need to feel okay again." Gently, very gently he holds me and I ball his shirt into my one good fist. But tears don't come and I slowly pull away, still trying to steady my trembling body. We sit in silence, our eyes locked, and it's all I need. I don't need his promises or words of comfort; I just need this moment, this clarity that he's here and always will be. I put my hand over his heart in thanks and then get shakily to my feet.

"We need to go."

We move on at a quicker pace; my breakdown has cost us considerable time. Jake needs me. I won't let him down, not when he has lost so much already.

At the outskirts of Fernhile, we pause and assess the risk of threat. As it's such a small town the security is minimal. We approach a GDO jeep and are beginning to open the door when a voice shouts.

"Hey! What do you think you're doing?!" My recent rebellious actions make me well practiced in delivering an easy lie.

"Our camp was attacked!" I point at my ripped uniform. "Our captain needs us to warn the lot up in Amphora. We need reinforcements!" He steps closer and examines my uniform.

"Can I help?"

"No, you stay here and keep control of this area. It's total chaos out there." He nods and steps back.

We jump into the jeep and speed away, Luca shaking his head in disbelief as he drives.

"Right? How dumb was he?"

"It's not him that amazes me. Your ability to cast a believable lie is frightening." I almost feel like smiling, which I didn't think would be possible at a time like this.

"Well, let's keep up with the lie that we need to warn our captain — it'll get us into the city easier." Luca nods.

The only other cars we pass are GDO ones, probably frantically being deployed to control pockets of chaos around the area. When it's empty the road reminds me of before the invasion, before everything began to collapse. Long drives home in the dark after weekends away at the lakes in the summer or ski trips in the winter, whilst I dozed in the back and my parents talked in hushed tones in the front. Peaceful, that's what I remember feeling, peaceful. I try to grasp at that feeling and recapture it but I can't; it slithers and fades away from me. I wonder if I will ever feel that way again.

Luca is driving fast and so we reach Amphora in no time at all. As we approach the city we can see fires burning all over the horizon. My heart hammers, and I hope we're not too late, hoping that one of those fires isn't Jake's doing.

There's a barricade up across the main access road to the centre of the city.

"We have word for our major about the Camburg camp."

"What's the news?" The soldier puffs himself up.

Luca leans out from the driver's window. "Get out of my way, private."

His low growl makes him sound incredibly menacing; I don't think I've ever heard Luca sound menacing, ever. The soldier steps back, saluting, and lets us through.

"Nice work, soldier."

"Learnt from the best." He smiles before his face settles back into hard determination as we race along the roads towards the GDO headquarters. Small riots are being held back by rings of GDO soldiers. A few cans and possibly bricks are thrown at our jeep as we go by. There are bodies in the streets and I look at them with the grim realisation that I have been the cause of this. I have been the reason that they died, all because I wanted to free my dad. Nausea rolls around my stomach. What have I done?

I don't get time to dwell on it because we've reached the headquarters and there are soldiers circling the entire building as a human barricade. I approach one.

"Who's in there?"

"The council." The war council, GDO's top officials for Auria.

"Anyone else?"

"Some civilians have taken shelter in the lobby."

I swear and go back to Luca.

"Do we know his point of entry?"

"No." Luca looks worried. How are we going to stop him?

"Okay, first we have to get the civilians out, and then the council."

Luca's eyebrows lift up to his hairline.

"I don't like them either but I'm not having my best friend executed for murder!"

"Okay, fair enough." Luca and I run back to the building.

"There's a bomb threat on this building, we have to get everyone out," I yell at the first soldier I approach.

The soldier looks sceptical. "Who are you?" Fortunately, throughout all of this, my lanyard is still around my neck; I hold it up to his face.

"Intelligence. I've just had to drive from Camburg because our communications are down; the town is overrun with rebels. Now get those people out. Now." I make sure I enunciate my words precisely. He looks across at his fellow soldier who seems decidedly panicked. I doubt he wants to be within the blast radius. Irritated, I push them to the side and barge in.

"You all need to leave. Now."

The crowd of people look up in shock but don't budge. Luca comes up behind me.

"There's a bomb," he bellows, and then all hell breaks loose.

"Really?" I yell above the din of people screaming and running at me. "Creating a panic was the best option?"

"It got them to move, didn't it?"

Fair enough — then I notice two people going against the crowd. I elbow Luc and point. Yve has dyed her hair black but I can tell it's her, and Jake has a cap on. Fury lights up inside me — they are going to go ahead with their plan even with all these people inside the building. I sprint towards them, flinging people aside as I go. Without thinking, I throw myself at Jake. We skid across the marble floor and land against the wall by the lifts, my wrist screaming. If I'm not careful I will actually break it.

"Cassia?!" He pushes me off him, he definitely wasn't expecting to see me. "What the hell are you doing?"

His face settles back into its adopted scowl.

"What the hell are *you* doing? Those are innocents over there!"

His eyes darken. "I wasn't going to do it on this floor."

"What, and you thought that a bomb on the fifth floor wouldn't bring the building down on top of them?"

"I was going to get them out —"

I look at him with disgust. "Enough of this, it's too dangerous."

He pulls away from me. "Get away from me, Crone."

His words sting. He knows I'm not one of them but he has become too bitter. When did he change so much?

"Don't do this, Jake."

He ignores me and gets up and walks to the lift. Yve and Luca stand beside me.

"Jake, let's go, Cassia's right. There are other ways." Yve's voice is soft, but pleading. He presses the button for the lift. Shaking, I pull Jono's ES gun from my belt.

"Jake." He looks at me with such hatred that my heart breaks as I fire, but I'm not quick enough; the lift doors have already opened and he's inside. The jolt flies past him and sets off sparks against the far wall. I scream and run towards him but the doors close. I race to the end of the bank of lifts and yank open the door to the stairwell and sprint for my life, for his life, up the stairs. I take them two at a time not noticing if the others are behind me, not caring if we're being pursued by the soldiers.

When I reach the fifth floor I'm slightly dizzy from running in a spiral and my breathing is laboured. Through the frosted glass panelling I can see the council standing around a table yelling. Jake's hooked a chain around the door handle and secured it around a nearby pillar. Two men are trying to open the door, another begins to swing a chair against the toughened glass, and a guard lies unconscious on the floor. The door to the neighbouring meeting room is ajar. I creep up, not wanting to alert the council to my presence.

Jake is on the floor with his backpack open and a mess of wires and plastic explosives is nestled inside. I step forward to stop him but he's already armed it. I freeze.

"Jake, disarm it before it's too late," I whisper.

"Get out of here, Cassia."

"I'm not going anywhere until you disarm that bomb."

He yanks me by the arm and drags me out of the room.

"You have to go."

"What were you planning on doing?"

He falters.

"You… you were going to stay? You… why?"

"I want them to know why, in their last seconds I want them to know that they're going to die, I want them to be afraid and for them to feel the fear and horror of what they've done."

"No. We have to go. You are not dying tonight." I begin to fight him. I'm tired and my wrist throbs but I have to get him to disarm the bomb; I have to get him to leave. He drags me out of sight of the meeting room to the lifts.

"Jake, we have to go."

He's holding me by my throat and I feel my mind swarming back to a few hours earlier when Kohler attacked me. I begin to flail in fear, my mind unable to react appropriately. The steel doesn't leave Jake's eyes but I can tell he's confused by my reaction.

"Jake."

He senses my hysteria because he loosens his grip. He looks at his watch and I notice a rising panic in him as he presses the lift button.

"There's no time to disarm the bomb now." He sounds almost apologetic.

"We have to go, we *have* to go." I'm pulling on his arm but he pushes me off. "What about your sister?"

He turns to me burning with pain and hatred. "I'm doing this for her."

"No, she wouldn't want this." I hear the doors roll open before I realise what he's doing. He throws me into the back of the lift and I'm screaming for him to come with me. The council have managed to get out of the meeting room and they are running towards us. He turns and presses the button for the ground floor. I scream for him to get in the lift but he just looks at me, fire burning in his eyes and a small smile on his lips.

"Goodbye," he mouths, as the doors begin to shut. He turns to face the council, words of revenge spilling from him — and I rocket forward to grab him, just as the hallway erupts into flames.

I'm tossed to the back of the lift and the doors shut and the lift sinks as the building rocks and wheezes and shatters around me.

Down and down and down.

I don't know if the lift is going too fast. And then it stops and the emergency lights go on. I am between floors. I don't want to move. I don't care about anything at that moment but then I hear Luca's voice calling to me, calling me back. I crawl to the doors and look up. I'm trapped between the first and second floor. I rest my head on the metal doors, which feel surprisingly cool. *Get out.* But I can't, I'm incapable of fighting. *Get out.*

I bang my fist on the doors, and using the last of my strength I yell for Luca. In no time at all he's on the other side of the door and he's somehow opening them. Ashen air floats in as he manages to get them apart enough for me to crawl through the small space between the floors. Yve is with him, helping hold it open. She looks around confused; she's looking for Jake. I don't want to meet her eyes but I owe her that at least. I don't need to say anything; once she looks at me she knows, and she begins to tremble.

Luca drags me outside as the building groans around us. At a safe distance we look back as the flames lick their way up the sides of the building. My legs collapse beneath me.

Life is so painfully fleeting; it can just be taken, without warning. In one moment everything you love is gone, and it is inconceivable. How can so much life just vanish? How can that smile just be gone, be nothing? As my tears fall my pain swells until it consumes my body and there is nothing but deep agony. But this time… this time I'd seen the signs. I am so angry with myself for not stopping him, so full of regret and white rage.

Memories of him begin to crowd my mind, each one forcing itself to be remembered first. Each one like a fresh blade to my heart, and each one making his death even more unfathomable. He can't be gone, he just can't. But he is. This is my reality. This is my horrible truth. I couldn't stop him. I couldn't save him, and it aches and it burns and it twists inside of me.

It takes me a while to realise Luca is holding me up, that my voice is hoarse and my tears invisible.

"We have to go," he whispers. I manage a nod and let him lead Yve and I to our jeep. Soldiers swarm around us in panic. No one notices us.

We drive out of the city without any problems; now that the council has been destroyed there's confusion everywhere, but a couple of miles outside the city we hit a road block. We tell Yve to get down in the back, hoping they won't spot her. Luca speaks to the guard.

"What's the problem?" I ask, as I lean over.

"There's been a prison break in Camburg."

"Oh, shit."

"Where've you two been?"

"Just left the city to go to our base. It's a mess out there."

"Tell me about it."

He is just about to wave us through when a man climbs out of the back seat of one of the jeeps. My body tenses instantly. Kohler. There is no way out of this now. I smile at the soldier and lean back in my seat and whisper to Yve, "Whenever you can, make a break for it, head north, and get to Vayo. Get out of here, okay?"

"Okay," she whispers back. I look at the blockade. There's no way we can fight our way through; there really is no option. I am about to be left in the hands of my most feared enemy.

I give Luca a sad smile and a gentle kiss. "This is it."

As I lean forward I slip the drives out of my pocket. I put Black Plague into Yve's hand, and slip Burnout into my bra.

"No, we can find a way."

"If we run we'll be shot. There is no other way." I brush my hand across his cheek.

"I won't let him hurt you anymore."

"He won't — look." Behind Kohler walks our major. Major Burgin is average height, maybe 5' 9", dark, receding hair clipped short, a slightly beaked nose, and permanently rosy cheeks. Had you seen him in jeans and a t-shirt you'd probably think nothing much of him but, when he wants to be, the man is terrifying.

Whilst the soldier nearest to us is distracted I explain the plan in a hoarse whisper. "Whatever they ask, just say that you helped me get out of Camburg because of what Kohler did and because we knew about the bomb threat — you were trying to protect me. Okay?"

"Okay."

"And no matter what they say, I will *never* give you up." I kiss him hard once.

He tangles his fingers in my hair. "If he touches you, do *whatever* it takes to make him stop. You hear me? Do not let him touch you." I nod, I will not let him touch me again.

I keep my eyes to the front not wanting to alert them to Yve's presence. The Major approaches first.

"Fortis, Kemei, get out of the car." We do as we're told, I leave my door open for Yve. Major Burgin isn't someone you disobey and we really are outnumbered.

"Where have you been?"

"Amphora," I reply.

"This truck was taken from near Fernhile."

"We left Camburg through the woods." Luca takes a step closer to me as he speaks.

"And then you headed to Amphora. What about the prisoners?" Burgin sounds sceptical.

"What prisoners? The system went down just as I got an alert saying there would be an attack on the headquarters and so I told Luca, I mean Kemei, we had to get there," I reply.

"And why didn't tell your captain?" He sounds sceptical; he must know about our plans but he's playing along, for the moment. I look down at the floor and Luca puts his hand in mine. It's strange; I am trying to make him believe that I have been attacked by Kohler, like it was a story I've made up, even though it isn't.

"Captain Kohler says he tried to stop you from freeing prisoners."

I look up and my eyes flash with rage. "That is *not* what happened."

Luca glares at Kohler with disgust. Major Burgin seems to take in my appearance for the first time. My ripped shirt, my matted hair and my torn trousers. He sighs. "You're both coming with me back to Camburg — you too, Kohler." Kohler's expression is murderous.

"Major, these two were involved in the prison break. You need to arrest them immediately."

Whilst Kohler is shouting I sense a movement behind me. Yve is making her move.

"Captain, I suggest you cool down and we'll talk about this back at the base." The atmosphere is calming down too quickly; there won't be enough of a distraction for Yve to get away.

"Major, please can we ride separately from him?" I make my voice shake. I mean, it probably would shake anyway but I'm really trying to hammer home that we are in no way involved in the prison break. And I'll keep lying about it, even if they have concrete evidence.

Kohler scoffs. He's still drunk and so I know that any comment from me will bring out a reaction.

"Major, this girl is a conniving little bitch. She seduced me. It must have been part of their plan. She cohorts with known rebels!"

I don't expect Luca to react; I haven't really thought about how this is affecting him. I know he hates Kohler for what he did but I assume he'll be his usual calm self. Not this time. This time, Luca lunges for Kohler. Two men jump in to hold him back, but Luca is too quick. Kohler stands rooted, completely shocked as Luca swings at him with a right hook that has so much rage and power behind it that Kohler is floored. It's hard for me to hold back a yell of triumph.

The Major roars with fury, "I do not have *time* for this! The entire country is in chaos!" He turns to his soldiers and barked orders. "Get them all into cars. *Separate* cars."

As I am being led away, my hands tied, I looked around but can't see Yve anywhere.

Walking back through the streets of Camburg makes me feel both elated and terrified. It's eerie after the chaos of the rest of the evening, but at least the people I care about are free, except for Luca that is. The darkness is profuse on the streets and the haunting feeling swells inside me. I have led Luca to doom; I can feel it with so much certainty. Luca will die because of me, just as Jake has done. Tears burn their way down my cheeks as I think of Jake, of the people dying at that moment because of a chain of events that I've started. I don't bother to hide them; I let them fall as the sound of our footsteps are muffled by the nothingness around us.

Major Burgin locks Luca and I in an interrogation room back in Camburg's old police station. Luca kneels in front of me as the silent tears keep falling. He wipes them away with his thumbs as he cups my face in his hands and kisses me softly on my forehead. The tenderness of it shatters me just a little bit more; I no longer know how I am even sitting up, how I am even breathing with the pain of it all. Both of us know not to speak, that we're being watched, that they're listening. Eventually, my tears stop. A guard brings us bottles of water but I don't recognise him; he's not based in Camburg.

Luca and I sit next to each other, my head on his shoulder, his resting against my head. I feel myself begin to drift off. It must be early in the morning and I can't fight the exhaustion any more. My eyes aren't closed for long — Major Burgin enters the room. I jolt awake instantly, blinking away the blurriness of sleep.

"So if your story is to be believed, you two chose a hell of a night to go AWOL."

"Sir, we weren't going AWOL, we were trying to get to Amphora to stop the headquarters being bombed." I keep my voice official; this isn't a time to be emotional.

"I checked into it and I can confirm reports from the soldiers there that you both charged in to stop the blast. It's a shame you failed."

I look down and nod, trying to hide how much I didn't want the bomb to go off. I can't let him know it was affecting me personally. I can't raise any suspicion.

"What I don't understand is why you didn't alert us here first."

I take a breath, steadying myself. "I had seen something on the alerts and was reading it when Captain Kohler came in and instructed me to see him in his office. I was going to tell the base because I didn't trust him. He'd been acting suspiciously, and I thought that maybe he was a mole for the rebels… when he… when he…" My voice catches and Luca grips my hand. I lift my chin and look the Major in the eyes.

"I fought Captain Kohler off. I scratched his face and incapacitated him and then ran to find Luca. I just had to get out of Camburg. Luca was worried about me so agreed to go into the woods with me. There weren't any guards on the gate, which was strange but it didn't really register at the time." Luca nods along with me. "In the woods I started to calm down and I remembered what I had found out. That's when we decided to go to Amphora, but I couldn't face going back into Camburg, I was worried what the Captain might do." I stop and wait. I look at the Major directly, knowing that my open expression will show him the truth. Kohler did attack me. I had run to the woods. We had gone to stop a bomb in Amphora. There is so much truth within the story that he can't not believe me.

The Major nods slowly and looks at Luca. "You left with her? Just like that?"

"Of course I did. I could see what had happened." He nods again, seemingly accepting our relationship as confirmation of that fact.

"And what do you know of the prison break here?"

I shrug as I look at Luca. "Nothing, sir."

"Nothing," Luca says.

The Major scrutinises us further. "I want you two to come with me."

He stands up and leads us out of the room. Two guards follow as we pass through the old station and outside, where the first light of the day is dusting gold across the barren streets. The last of the mist sits low by the gates of Camburg, swirling menacingly. We follow the Major to the radio station, into the Intelligence building. Inside, Jaidee is sweating with a guard standing very close behind him. He looks up as we enter and gives me a panicked look.

"What's happened, Jaidee?" I ask, keeping a note of surprise in my voice.

"Everything's fried."

"What? How?"

The Major holds up his hand silencing me. "Fortis, I am the one asking questions here. You were on duty that night and I understand you were the only one awake."

"That's correct, sir."

He nods and continues. "You said you saw an alert come through about Amphora?"

"Yes, sir."

"I've spoken to our office in Amphora and they didn't put anything through."

I try to steady my breathing, desperate not to give myself away. "Let me show you on the system what I saw." I go to the computer and stop. "Oh, right…" I pause as if I've just remembered everything is down. Seriously, I'm on my way to getting an award for liar of the year.

"What I want to know, Fortis, is how you knew about the attack in Amphora."

I turn back to the Major and look at him earnestly. "I don't know… Maybe… maybe one of the rebels sent out the alert, you know, sometimes terrorist groups do that?" I shrug with false confusion.

Major Burgin rocks back on his heels, eying me carefully. He suspects me, but he must have his doubts about Kohler not to have locked me up straight away. At that moment, Jaidee slams his fist down in frustration.

"Can I help?" I ask, dutifully.

"No, the system overheated and everything is fried. Not only that, but apparently the entire network is down as well. I just can't see how the two are related but man, it's a weird coincidence."

"Could the overheating have happened because of whatever brought the network down?"

I am pretty sure I am doe-eyed at this point. Maybe I am starting to over-milk the innocent act.

"No, I don't see how."

Luca is desperately trying to hide his discomfort. We're in a precarious position, with so much resting on them not realising the source of the crash came from here.

A messenger comes for the Major and whispers in his ear. "Fortis, Kemei, stay here." He points to the two guards near the door. "You two come with me."

He leaves us with Jaidee and his guard, who eyes us with suspicion. When the Major has been gone five minutes I request a toilet break — the soldier isn't sure who to watch, and I notice his hesitation.

"The toilet is just round the corner, I won't be far. Please, they haven't let me pee for like six hours. I seriously have to go."

He still looks unsure and when a man is unsure you just have to make them uncomfortable. "Look, I really have to go, you know. *Female* stuff. It's a pretty bad situation." He relents, blooming red. Menstruation; every man's weakness.

I turn right instead of left, trusting that the soldier is too embarrassed to look at me. I creep carefully to Kohler's office — the door is open and the room empty. Removing the USB from my bra

I wipe it with my sleeves as I scan the room. His wooden desk is too obvious and there isn't an air-conditioning vent. Nothing. I begin to panic and look up to the heavens to help. Heaven helps me; the ceilings are those polystyrene tiles that can be pushed up, the hiding place for all contraband in schools across the nation. Balancing carefully on Kohler's swivel chair I carefully push up a tile above his desk and, making sure I'm holding it with my jumper, I slip the drive into the gap. I manage to get back down the hall and take the opportunity to actually use the toilet — I wasn't lying about the lack of toilet breaks.

"Wow, thanks man, I feel sooo much better." I grin at the soldier who looks away and shifts uncomfortably.

I give Luca what I hope is a meaningful look; he seems to twig that I have done something in our interest but not what.

Eventually Burgin comes back. "I'm keeping you two detained for now, until I know more."

"Yes, sir." Luca stands up straight. Such the dedicated soldier. If I was Burgin, I would never have suspected Luca.

"Umm, sir, will we be allowed a meal?" I bite my lip, I don't know who this master manipulator and lip biter is, but I need to eat something before I pass out.

"I'll have food sent to your cells."

"Thank you, sir."

As we leave the Intelligence room, Luca elbows me lightly. I mouth, "What?" to him. We need to keep our strength up and thinking about food is better than thinking about everything else. I need to stay alert, stay focused, and I can't think about Jake or the others. I have to think about saving Luca, because that's what matters right now.

WEEK THIRTEEN

Sunday comes and goes. So does Monday. Tuesday is an equally dull day. Luca and I are now kept in separate cells and we can't see or hear one another, but I know he's near and nothing has happened to him because I can hear when his food is delivered. The walls in my cell are grey, the white and grey striped mattress yellowed. The pillow is thin and inconsequential; the sheet looks like it has decade old blood and whatever else stains ingrained into it. I choose not to use it. My steel toilet and sink make me grateful that I'm in a cell alone.

When the small rays of sunshine break into my cell I think of my parents in safety, Yve meeting up with them, Luca getting out and joining them but without the light fire dances in my eyes, Jake's hand, an explosion. I cry every night but not during daylight hours because if I do I will break and I have to stay strong for Luca. Our fabricated story is keeping us alive.

Finally, on Wednesday morning I'm summoned to the same interview room I'd been in on my first night back, and once again I tell Major Burgin what happened. I imagine Luca's doing the same, but I know he won't betray me. Neither one of us will break. I'm then returned to my cell.

Patience, I just need patience. Kohler was feeding them intelligence on me; I can turn it so that he seems the real traitor. The cameras were down so they can't place me at the prison break, or Luca for that matter. Luca was on duty with Simon so there were no witnesses outside the prison. Our only problem is the guards who were inside the prison; had any of them recognised us? I have to believe there was too much chaos for them to have paid much attention to who was assisting in the prison break.

This realisation makes me pray, something I haven't done in a while. I mean, why bother when your mother is dying of cancer, your father is incarcerated, and your nation has been occupied by an evil superpower? But, that night I decide it's time to try for some divine intervention because Luca was at the prison break before me, he would have confronted the guards in there, never expecting to come back and face the music. The realisation that Luca could be in more trouble than me brings me to my knees, and I pray. I pray to God in an angry voice — *enough is enough, give us a break. Luca's a good guy!* As I am yelling at God in my head the door to my cell clicks unlocked. I open one eye to the sky. "Fast work, old man," I mutter.

I am led, chained, once again to Major Burgin's office; Luca is sitting in front of him. I am pushed down into the free chair. I chance a look at Luca, and he seems well. Nervous, but well.

"I have come to a decision." I count my heartbeats as I wait for him to come to the point.

"Despite your claims that Kohler was incriminating you in his stead, I have confirmation that both of you were seen at the prison break out. And for that matter I don't believe you went to stop a bomb, I believe you planted one that killed senior GDO officials." I hold back a curse aimed directly at God; I really thought he'd be on my side with this one. I keep silent and feel the slightest change in Luca's demeanour. "You will both be held here for the time being until I've confirmation on how to deal with you."

My mind races. Protesting our innocence over the bombing in Amphora won't help us at this point. I need to think of a strategy that diverts the blame to Kohler. How can I get them to find the evidence planted in Kohler's office? Nothing. I am coming up with nothing. If I drop any hints, I am automatically implicating myself. I have completely forgotten about my partner in crime, whose mind is clearly working faster than mine. As the Major is readying to leave the room Luca speaks. "What about Kohler?"

"What about him?" The Major sounds tired and impatient.

"He attacked Cassia."

"And he will be dealt with."

Luca is trying to contain himself; I can see he's beginning to lose his own battle. I let my hand fall over his. We'll worry about Kohler another day. Right now we are staring into the face of a court martial, and in the GDO that usually means the old-fashioned kind — a shot to the head. At this point the best thing for us to do is shut up. We'll just have to wait and pray that we can figure a way out of this mess with the evidence I planted and testimonials from guards in Amphora, or we'll have to try and escape. Option number two is a lot worse; breaking in to a prison is one thing, breaking out seems like an impossible task. Luckily, because of the damage to the main building we are still being held at the police station. It's our only advantage at this point.

WEEK FOURTEEN

Not much has changed since the Major decided we're guilty. Four more days in a cell with nothing to do. No interactions with anyone else; just me, in a cell, with the occasional meal. At least I am already used to the food. I still wake every morning with the hollowness of loss, I still replay the night in the GDO headquarters wondering what I could have done differently. And then, like a skipping track, the moment of the explosion, of the lift doors closing, plays over and over again. Jake saying goodbye, the way his t-shirt was slightly bunched to one side from when I was pulling at his arm. I can't stop thinking about his stupid t-shirt, the one that was soft from wear, the one that smelled of him, even when it had just been washed and he'd lent it to me to sleep in.

Without a distraction from the pain, the rawness intensifies and I realise the conditions in the prison won't kill me; the loneliness will. I try to keep reminding myself of all the people I care about who are safe now, who are free, but my self-torture reminds me that they aren't free, they are on the run. Maybe they've all been captured too. And what about Mateo and his family? Are they in prison? Are they even alive? And Luca, what about him? The guilt, the loss, the loneliness spiral around me. My second week in prison is my darkest.

WEEK FIFTEEN

At the start of my third week I wake up with a new determination; I won't allow myself to be defeated. I was psychologically torturing myself and I need to be mentally prepared for whatever comes next. I begin a routine. I move my bed so that the first strips of sunlight fall across my eyes, giving me an early start. I do sit-ups, push-ups (seeing as my wrist is pretty much healed — not fractured after all), and burpees. I jump up onto my bed and down again until I am sweating and exhausted. Then I'm taken out for my only walk of the day, to the shower down the hall. I wash, then back in my cell I have my breakfast. I take my time over it, draw it out. After breakfast I sit with my body bathed in sunlight, despite the heat, and think of a plan. I already know the rough layout of the old police station and guard rotation, thanks to my time staring at security monitors. I just need to look for weaknesses, which I do on my daily trips to the shower.

I've figured out where Luca's cell is as well. I can't see in. Our doors are metal with small flaps through which our food is posted, but I know which is his. I decide to let him know I'm okay by singing "Dreamers Day", a terrible pop song we'd sing when cleaning the streets to cheer ourselves up. It used to really get on Luca's nerves, but I could tell he enjoyed Jake and I messing about singing it.

> *Dreaming on a Sunday*
> *That Monday won't come at all*
> *Drink champagne on ice*
> *You'll never hear the alarm call*
>
> *Dreaming for tomorrow*
> *Where today is gone*
> *With toes in the sand*
> *And the drinks flow on and on*

I sing softly as I walk to the shower. The first time is hard as it makes me think of Jake; I carry on as it's also a way of me working out timings to a rhythm. I reach the chorus by the door to the bathroom, humming it under my breath whilst I wash, and on my third round and on the second verse, I'm back out of the shower and there's only one guard in the hall; the other guard reappears at the end of the chorus. It's a system and it's hopefully a little sign for Luca, something to keep his spirits up.

On what must have been the Wednesday of that week, I hear a soft baritone singing:

I asked of hope to the giver
He said it wasn't time
We went down to the river
And threw ourselves a line

When I was home sleepin'
He hollered at me and said
"Son, the tide is changin'"
And to the ocean we fled

We came upon the water
And cast out our net
Then waited 'til we caught her
But she flailed and she fret

He said, Son, you can keep her,
If your soul says so
But I said, "Daddy,
I gotta let the mermaid go"

I waded to the water
And let the spirit free
"Son, you freed Earth's daughter"
And peace came to me

It's a song I'm used to hearing him sing to himself, in the evenings at his house. It used to lull me to sleep and I told him one night in our dorm that it was one of my favourite memories. The comfort I feel from his soft, deep voice drifting through the perpetual grey of my cell is so overwhelming I have to bury my eyes in my hands just so I can focus on that sound even more, so that I can hold it to me, breathe it, and allow it to bring me strength.

We're stronger because we have each other, and in that moment I know I can get through anything with him nearby.

Using my thumbnail, I begin to map out what I've seen and what I remember of the basement holding cells layout. I draw on the floor, under my bed so it won't be spotted. There are seven doors I have to open to free both Luca and me, eight cameras, and two guards. It used to be at least three, but numbers are down. It's an old cell block and so the doors are key-operated, which works in our favour. The basement level might be achievable, but the ground floor is a different story.

Unfortunately for us, the red light I noticed the day before means that the security cameras are back online. What I do know though, is that I have to be prepared because an opportunity could present itself at any moment.

And then, two days later, it does.

I am waiting by the door to my cell, ready to be escorted out. The door opens and my guard for the day, who I think of as Steve although he won't tell me his name (a fed-up-looking man in his mid-forties who hasn't kept up with his training and who is clearly finding the humidity unbearable) leads me out into the hall. He's fumbling with my cuffs, his keys are on his belt, and there isn't another guard in sight. Opportunity.

I thrust upwards with my wrist and break his nose, sweep his legs out from under him, and when he falls, kneel down on his chest. I put my hand over his mouth and I whip and twist my towel into a makeshift gag. I tie it round his head and stuff the fat part into his open mouth, all the while pinning his shoulders down with my knee. Grabbing his cuffs, I flip him onto his front and lock them onto his wrists. I drag him, with a lot of effort, into my cell and away from the cameras. No alarm has yet been sounded, which means whoever is on duty isn't doing their job. I grab the keys from his belt loop and check the cameras. I count to four, giving me the opportunity of a momentary blind spot, and dart across and down the hall to Luca's cell. I try five keys before the lock tumbles open.

Luca is doing push-ups when the door swings open.

"Fancy going for a run?" He leaps up, kisses me hard and fast and follows my lead down the hall. If the army has taught us anything, it's that we can spring to action without any prompting. The third door I reach I unlock quicker, and the fourth, at the top of the stairs to the ground floor, is already open. Security is really getting lax. You'd think with them suspecting us of a prison break they'd keep a better eye on us.

There is no point worrying about the cameras at this stage; we just need to get out. Luca peers around the corner and holds up two fingers. Two guards. One for each of us. He drops to a crouch and I follow suit, trying not to get distracted by his taut muscles glistening with sweat. Time and place Cassia, time and place. He makes a move forward and I follow. The guards see us but too late, we're already in position. I take the one who was sitting down, and holding one hand over their mouths and wrapping our arms around their necks, we hold on until they go limp then lower them to the floor.

I look up into the security booth. No one has seen us because one of the guards, who was supposed to be monitoring us, has been chatting with his buddy and we've already taken care of him. Honestly, how the GDO conquered entire nations sometimes astounds me. I make my way into the booth and release the two electronic doors. Luca props one open and holds the other one for me. At the last set of doors, we stop.

"What's the plan?" Luca looks to me.

"Remember in training how we had to break in to a compound?"

"You want us to break out the same way?" He smiles at me.

"You've got it, soldier. No matter what, we need to keep moving."

I put my hand to the handle; this door wouldn't be locked.

"The most direct route there?"

"Absolutely." I open the door a few inches and check our surroundings; the street in front of us has a few people going about their daily routine. A couple of soldiers are patrolling the streets. We need to blend in and fortunately we're not in prison clothes, just combat trousers and vests, so we can easily pass as off-duty soldiers.

"Act natural." Luca takes my hand and we walk out and start up an inane conversation. We cut left down a side alley and take a fire escape up to the roof.

"Do we run low, crawl? What do you think is best?" I squint at Luca as I ask. The sun is behind him giving him an angelic halo.

"Run low, we're less likely to slip and draw attention. Best keep noise to a minimum."

I nod and pull him into a kiss. "The messes I get you in to."

"It's why I love you."

Thinking about it, escaping prison together and sitting on a rooftop *is* probably the most romantic time to tell someone that you love them; Luca is excellent at finding his moments.

"And the fact that you put up with it is why I love you too." He gives me one of his smiles that shows all his teeth and makes the world tilt further on its axis, and then begins to move.

At the end of the building, we pause. The jump isn't far but the noise of impact will definitely draw attention.

"When you make it to the roof, just run. Don't look back or hesitate. You run."

I take a breath and walk back a few paces, run, and vault. The air is sucked from my lungs as I fling myself across the gap and I land on my feet, my hands cartwheeling as I try not to topple back. Once I regain my balance, I push forward and hear Luca land behind me. We run, our feet scrabbling across the slate-tiled, pitched roof. I hear shouts and I increase my pace. The fence isn't far; we're almost there. I am about to jump down and out over the fence when the crack of a gun stops me. I spin to check on Luca and I know from the look on his face that he's hit. It's not pain I see; it's regret. I race forward and check his torso and then see the blood pooling from his thigh. I pull him down to minimise us as targets as bullets begin to shatter tiles around us.

"We have to keep moving. You can do this."

"No." He sounds so earnest it hurts. "You have to go without me. We'll get caught if I come, I'll slow us down."

"I am *not* leaving you."

I pull off his shirt from over his head and check the back of his leg. There's no exit wound. I ball his top up and hold it to his thigh. He winces in pain.

"Bullet still in there?"

"So you can keep it as a souvenir from 'the time we escaped from prison.'"

He lets out a quiet laugh.

"Going to be a good story is it?" I lean forward and kiss his cheek.

"The best."

I turn to see a couple of soldiers coming across the roof, their guns trained on us.

"Time to get moving."

Luca shakes his head. "Cass, today isn't our win."

"But it has to be."

He holds my cheek gently in his hand. "One day soon, but not today."

I know he's right. We're not getting away now, but I don't want to give up, not whilst I'm under the open sky.

"This is just our dress rehearsal then?"

"Exactly. Next time I'll remember not to get shot in the leg."

The soldiers are on us now and Luca raises his hands. I raise one, the other still staunching the bleeding from his leg.

"Nice shot, was that you, Hermandez?" Luca looks up at the Utonian guard.

"Payback for beating me at cards." Hermandez doesn't smile; it takes a lot to shoot and arrest a friend. "Do me a favour and don't make this difficult, okay?" He kneels down and cuffs us both.

"No problem, just try and make sure one of you keeps pressure on his leg."

"Sure thing, Fortis."

Getting Luca down off the roof isn't easy but they manage it and stretcher him away. I am led back to the jail block where Luca's blood is showered off me by a pissed-off looking guard, before I'm put back into my cell. My legs are shackled this time and they don't remove them when they lock my door.

When the sun goes down that evening, I don't cry.

WEEK SIXTEEN

It's Monday morning. I know, because I've been keeping track. I am taken from my cell before I have a chance to work out, and led by four armed guards to the barracks. They drop me off in what was once the headmaster's office to the old school but is now the Major's. Major Burgin is sitting behind his desk; Captain Becker and Captain Fleming stand behind him. On Burgin's desk is the flash drive I stashed in Kohler's office. I try not to react.

"Please remain standing, Fortis." I stand to attention and wait. "After a rigorous search, we found this flash drive among your personal effects." I don't bother to hide my astonishment.

"What? I don't understand?"

"They were found among your things in your room and it has been agreed that you shall be court-martialled for crimes against the Global Defence Organisation."

"No!" This can't be happening. I can't be found guilty. This isn't really happening.

"It's all the proof that we need. You will be presented in front of a firing squad on Wednesday at midday. Your boyfriend Luca, as a co-conspirator, will be by your side."

"But that's hardly proof — it must have been planted!"

Burgin leans forward. "Fortis, I looked through the list of prisoners we held. Imagine my surprise when I saw Antonio Fortis on the list. Kohler wasn't setting you up, was he?"

"Luca had nothing to do with it."

"The decision has been made."

I have no response. That's it. I am going to be executed. My vision blurs and I feel my body flare up with heat. "No!" I scream, over and over until I feel a stinging in my arm and I fall limp.

I've led Luca to his execution and there's nothing I can do to stop it.

I am numb all of Tuesday, out of options, out of hope. I don't want to die. And Luca; Luca will be dead because of me. He'll be executed. *Shot* because of me. I've done this.

The thought makes me retch.

I pace the room. Jake, now Luca. Jake and now Luca. Jake and Luca. Has any of it really been worth it? Have we made a difference at all? No. The GDO is still in power; we are just a group of stupid children who tried to fight a giant, and lost.

In the end, although I can't sleep, I just lie on my revolting mattress and stare at my cracked grey ceiling and will the night away. The sooner it's done, the sooner I will be free of my torment.

When the sun hits my face I am asleep. I sit up and watch as the light sneaks into the small space and slowly expand. I close my eyes and pray to a God that I don't believe in because I want to believe so badly, because believing might bring me some peace.

They still take me to my morning shower, but I don't sing on my way there. I leave Luca to his thoughts, if he's even in his cell and not in sick bay.

They feed me the same food as usual; no special requests on death row here. They do ask if I have any other last requests, although I get the impression they don't really mean to grant me a thing, and I ask to be allowed to wear my necklace when they execute me. I'm proud I am able to say "executed" without stammering or crying.

Just before 12pm I am collected from my cell by four guards and escorted outside, along the streets where people gawp, and to the front of the old town hall. They bring Luca and me from different directions so that we're face-to-face when we stand in front of the steps of the old building.

"I'm so sorry," I whisper.

He looks at me and with a sad smile he whispers, "I chose this, this isn't your fault."

A soldier approaches and clasps my necklace around my throat. Unshed tears shimmers in Luca's eye.

"I love you."

"I love you too." I look at the man that I love and all the hope and promise he gives me.

We're turned to face the fountain in the middle of the courtyard and from the corner of my eye I see the face of someone I will never forget. He approaches, bends down, and whispers in his hot, wet breath, "Happy birthday, Cassia."

I have forgotten it's my birthday; it hasn't even crossed my mind. I suppose it's Kohler's idea of sick justice that I die on my eighteenth birthday, but honestly, it comforts me. I've made it to eighteen, at least that's something.

Luca looks across at me; he knows what Kohler said but I shake my head and manage a smile. I'm okay, I'm telling him, it's okay. But what isn't okay is that Kohler has been let off. Somehow he found, or got someone to find, the evidence I'd planted and hid it back among my things.

Major Burgin stands before us in his ceremonial uniform. I'm grateful that he doesn't look smug, like Kohler does.

"Private Cassia Fortis and Private Luca Kemei, you have been found guilty of treason against the Global Defence Organisation and the people of this nation. You will be executed at gunpoint under the laws that you opposed."

There, in that moment, I know what it means to have the courage of your convictions. The GDO has to be held accountable for the killing of thousands, maybe even millions, of people. We may not have succeeded in our endeavour but at least we tried, and knowing that allows me to die at peace.

He turns and salutes the two marksmen who are our executioners. At least he hasn't allowed Kohler to be the one to pull the trigger, although I'm sure he asked — no, begged. He wouldn't have given off the professional air they desired though. To my left I notice they're filming us. Wonderful, our deaths are to be propaganda tools. Knowing that the camera is there gives me the courage I need. I won't whimper, cry, or beg for my life; I will die with dignity. It's all I have left that I can control.

I look over at Luca. "See you on the other side."

"Hopefully it's not as hot."

I laugh, despite myself, and turn towards my execution, a smile still on my face and a lightness in my heart that I didn't expect. The soldier that stands in front of me is doing his best to hide his terror; he's not much older than me. I feel sympathy for him, knowing he didn't want to do it, and I forgive him. Maybe my prayers to God have worked; maybe this is his influence, this feeling of total peace and forgiveness.

I'm ready.

The soldiers raise their guns and they take their aim, and I inhale in a slow, beautiful, last breath.

The air tastes curiously sweet.

I hear the bullets slot into their chambers and I slowly close my eyes…

and let death come.

But it doesn't. Has he missed? I open my eyes and look fearfully across to Luca, who is looking back at me with the same question on his face. I look at my executioner and he's on the floor cradling a bleeding hand, and Luca's guard is holding his arm and he appears to be bleeding from his calf muscle too.

And there's chaos.

People are yelling and screaming but I feel so detached from it all. I see Kohler fighting his way towards me, his gun drawn. He's about to take the shot when the butt of a rifle knocks him to the floor. The owner of the rifle charges towards me; he's Mediterranean-looking with dark hair lightly touched with grey, his features strong and masculine and, yes, handsome. Everything is incredibly vivid and yet distant at the same time. He has a beard that looks like it has been grown from lack of a razor rather than fashion; he has the air of a fighter, of a rescuer. That's when I know exactly what he is and that's when I come back to myself.

He stands before me and nods to someone at my back. I'm lifted to my feet and unshackled, and the moment Luca's free he's holding me in his arms; I never want to let go, but our saviour has other plans.

"Time for us to be going."

Luca pulls away and without hesitation we follow our rescuer. A short man with a receding hairline, who looks to be in his forties, thrusts a handgun into my hand and Luca is passed one as well. We run forward, towards the gates that lead out into the woods. Two guards stand at the exit looking panicked; one raises his rifle and by the look of him he'll pull the trigger out of fear rather than experience. Our liberator seems to realise this as well — he slows his pace and raises his hands, and we follow suit. Two men come from behind the guards and smash them over the head with their rifles — the soldiers crumple like paper dolls. The faces of our two new companions light me up — Jono and Drummer are grinning back at us.

"How've you been?" Drummer asks, casually.

"Oh, you know, on a diet," Luca responds. Laughing, we run towards them and hug them before our rescuer calls for us to get moving. We try and catch up as we run, but Luca's struggling with his leg.

"Are our parents well?" I ask, our general pace slower to account for Luca's injury.

"Worried about you, but other than that they're fine." Jono finds it hard to speak whilst running; he never kept up training once we were initiated.

"Did Yve find you?"

"The Amazonian, oh yeah, she found us." Jono whistles for good measure.

"Alright, alright." I smile as I run. The others are safe.

We don't go left towards the lake, instead we take a right-hand path that leads to a dirt road where a couple of jeeps are waiting, one with an open back.

"You two, in the front truck." Our rescuer points to Luca and me. "Jono, Drummer, I want you on the back of the second with your rifles ready. They'll not be far behind."

Of course, that's the moment we hear the pop of a gun; as one we duck and run to our respective jeeps. As soon as we're in, the driver puts his foot down. Our rescuer is with Luca in the back, with the man with a receding hairline.

I turn to him — "Thank you, for coming for us."

"I owed you a debt."

"Oh?" I have no idea what he's talking about.

"I'll explain later."

"Still, thanks… err."

"Dune." He replies.

"Thanks for coming for us, Dune." Luca slaps him on the back in a familiar way.

"And I'm Ian," says his companion. We exchange names and brief pleasantries, which seem out of place inside our getaway vehicle.

"Um, Luc?"

"Yeah?"

"Why does it seem like you know Dune?"

Luc looks uncomfortable. "I wanted to tell you and I'm really sorry that I didn't, but I didn't want to endanger you…"

"Well?"

"I met up with a small faction of rebel fighters when we were still living in Amphora, and joined up."

"What!"

He has the good grace to look guilty about his omission. "I wanted to tell you and I was going to, once we were in Vayo, but…"

"Then I got us captured. Okay, I'm mad you lied…"

Luca cuts me off. "I didn't lie, I just didn't tell you…"

I cut him off right back. "You *lied,* but considering you did it to avoid putting me in danger and I got you shot, captured, and almost court-martialled, I *may* forgive you." I am genuinely angry he didn't tell me but after everything, I don't have the energy to hold on to it.

Taking in a breath I turn to Dune. "Are we going to Vayo, are the other's still there?" I ask.

"They are, but we need to keep the GDO off our trail. We'll park the jeeps up and go the rest of the way on foot."

"That would explain why we're going in the wrong direction."

He smiles.

The road is hard to navigate. There are sharp turns and potholes and the driver, Dan, is having to drive too fast. We have already experienced a few almost–accidents, when the sound of gunfire starts up again.

"If we can't lose them, we can't go back to Vayo for a while." Dune looks at me as I turn. Keeping our families safe, that's what's important. I nod.

"Are they aware that may be an option?" I don't want the others thinking the worst.

"Yes, and we'll send someone to let them know where we go from there."

"It's a good plan," Luca interjects, and looks at me with understanding. We're not about to risk everyone else's lives just so we can feel comforted by being with our parents.

The gunfire doesn't stop as we bump along the forest tracks; I just hope Dune has a plan to get us out of this situation. What happens next is probably why I assume he's the leader of the group. He does have a plan.

Dan swerves right and goes off the trail through the forest; he dodges trees, barely, and keeps up a terrifying pace. Ahead there are tyre marks but he turns abruptly to the left, followed closely behind by the other truck. I look into the rear-view mirror and see ten men appear from the trees and they begin covering our tracks. The jeeps pull up behind some dense shrubs, and the engines are cut.

"The paths you made, where do they lead?" I ask.

"A ravine." Ruthless, but still a good plan. Quietly we leave our vehicles and help cover the cars in leafy branches.

Backpacks are pulled from the boot of our car and we each shoulder one, and then set out on foot towards the mountains. Luca limps beside me, using me as a crutch.

After an hour we're pretty sure we haven't been followed, but we'll be tracked. We stop for a rest, which I'm grateful for. Jono, Drummer, Luca, and I have a group hug — the troop finally back together.

Dune explains that the men and women we'd seen out on the road will catch up soon and we should wait. They're travelling behind us and covering the trail. Some, he says, were raised in the woods and know how to track and stay hidden. He has useful allies.

"How long have you been out here?" I ask.

"Since the beginning. I'd seen what they had done in other countries. When I knew they were coming here, I had to come home and do what I could."

"How come you were in other places they occupied?"

For the first time since I've met Dune, he seems unsure of himself. "I was a soldier, before all this." He sweeps his hand over imaginary devastation. "I fought for my country and then, when the situation changed, I deserted my regiment because I couldn't turn against my own people." It was a feeling I knew too well. "Fortunately, a lot of my men came with me."

"And Auria is your home?"

"Yes, I came for the Prime Minister."

"You freed her?" Luca asks.

"No, you both helped free her."

"Wait, we did? I didn't see her at the prison; I didn't even know she was held there."

Dune smiles and shakes his head in disbelief. "You released their most valuable prisoners and you didn't even realise. I can't decide if it was blind luck or if you're very effective spies."

"I dunno, I'd say it was more like dumb luck. We were fortunate that the others found gas canisters stored with the ES guns." I shrug.

"Cassia." Luca looks at me. "It was your plan, it was well thought out. The only reason we were caught…" He looks down, not wanting to say Jake's name, not wanting to open the wound.

"I heard about your friend, I'm sorry." I acknowledge Dune's sympathy but don't say anything; there isn't anything to say.

"So, what have you been doing out here?" I ask, to try and distract myself from the grief that throbs inside me.

"At first, building our forces, getting enough people together so that we could fight back. Then, we started hitting back at the GDO."

"You're the Resistance?" My eyes bulge; he's basically the hero to the people. "You started it?" He nods. A handsome, modest, hero; good thing he's too old for me.

"We'd managed to amass enough weapons to launch an attack on Camburg when we heard from an inner city group that a teenage girl had found a way to take down the security network and was going to free the Camburg prisoners." It's hard not to blush. "So, I sent a few men to watch over the break out — make sure everything went smoothly and to ensure the PM got out, whilst we freed our best asset and took the opportunity to strengthen our forces."

"And who is your best asset?" I lean forward, captivated.

"A female spy, like yourself, but she was discovered, well actually, more like betrayed, and was in a maximum security lock-up, but she's back with us and she has a lot of information that's going to help the Resistance."

I look at Luca and reach out for his hand. This is it; this is why we stood up to the GDO. We are going to help bring them down. We can become part of the Resistance.

"You've read the files from SINN?" I shift my attention back to Dune.

"Some." It's not hard to tell that what he saw he didn't like.

"Is there a plan?"

"Of sorts." He's grinning. He knows what my next question will be.

"Can we help?"

"Absolutely."

The group behind us appears from the trees as if they're apparitions, they're so silent. I've been distracted talking to Jono and Drummer, catching up on the rest of their journey to Vayo and finding Dune. Leading the group is a woman in loose-fitting army fatigues; her flame red dyed hair is tied back into a high ponytail that accentuates her cheek bones, and her green eyes shine brightly. Dune practically leaps from his seat when he sees her and draws her into a hug.

"All go well?"

"All well." He smiles affectionately at her.

"Echo, I'd like you to meet Cassia and Luca."

"The final two of the heroic four," she says, as she approaches with her hand extended.

"I like the sound of that." Jono claims the title proudly.

"We sound like characters from a children's story," Drummer grumbles.

"Sorry I couldn't be there to get you out, Dune doesn't think I'm 'combat ready'."

"Nothing a few good meals won't heal though." He smiles at her again and I try to work out if they're together or if he's head over heels without her realising.

"Here —" I hand her a bread roll from my pack — "to get you started." She winks at me and accepts the roll.

"We should really get moving. You good to go, or do you need a rest?" Dune asks Echo.

"No, I'm good. You're right, we should go. Five of the group will hang back and keep covering our tracks. I'll come up front with you and help keep an eye out."

Dune nods, not at all bothered that he's being bossed around, and we begin moving. What I like most about Dune and Echo is that they don't seem to see us as children. Instead, we're equals in their eyes, a couple more fighters to add to the Resistance.

We trek into the late afternoon and then stop for a rest. Luca's putting a brave face on it but I know that he must be in agony.

Echo sits down with Luca and me. "I'm really happy you guys want to help out, we could definitely use the manpower and people who have worked on the inside."

"Where were you based?" I ask.

"In Naevena, as a major. I was part of the army in my country — before — but our general chose to surrender his forces to the GDO. I decided to play the GDO loyalty card and worked my way up the ranks and fed information out to Dune, who I'd met when he was working with an "Aurian delegation" in Naevena. He was the first person I truly trusted." She glances briefly at Dune, then carries on, "I built up a good network of spies but one of them turned on me, someone I was very close to. It landed me in a lot of trouble." She smiles ruefully, the small traces of a broken heart evident in that look. My heart goes out to her.

"Does the network still stand?" I ask.

"Yes, well, I hope so. That's why I need to go back. We were close to finding out when the next meeting of the senior officials in Naevena would be, as the president of the GDO was going to be in attendance."

I suck in a breath — that's big. The president is never seen in public; it's rumoured he's terrified of an assassination attempt, which is probably an accurate assessment of how well hated he is. To find out where he'd be would mean that we'd have a chance of capturing him, of cutting off the head of the snake. We could actually bring about the end of the GDO.

"That's huge." Luca looks at Echo with respect.

"I'm hoping the intel you gathered will help us target him and other people in a senior position. First we need to weaken the GDO as a whole, which is where I think the Heroic Four," she smiles at Drummer, "will be needed. And, whilst we do that, we'll have people here building up the Resistance and government officials preparing to take the country back — all thanks to you guys."

With hope bubbling inside once again, we press on towards the mountains. As the light begins to soften we're halted and we all take a defensive position, hiding as best we can. A scouting party of five GDO soldiers step forward among us. Instantly, five of Dune's people jump out and silently fight the soldiers hand-to-hand, killing their opponents, one by one until only one is left alive.

I watch on in horror. We've been trained to kill but it doesn't mean I am willing to do it. Is this what I have just agreed to? The glow of hope feels tainted.

The survivor is brought before Dune, his hands tied behind his back. Dune leans on the man's shoulder, where it's bleeding. He groans with pain.

"How many more are following us?"

"I don't know."

Dune pulls out a knife, sticks the tip in the man's wound, and twists. He screams. I look away and Luca rests his hand on the small of my back.

"Two more groups of five; we split up." Dune looks him in the eye, accepts this as the truth, and then swiftly slips his blade across the man's throat; instantly my vision begins to blur. I have to take deep breaths to stop myself from vomiting. I bend low and watch the black wisps dissipate.

The bodies are quickly hidden and the area covered with leaves before we move on. I allow a distance to open up between everyone else and Luca, Jono, Drummer, and me.

"I don't know about this," I look at Luca.

"I know."

"Look, we've known them a few days longer than you have, they're good people. They're organised and they've got a network already in place." Jono looks at Drummer for his usual backup.

"I know what you saw was pretty brutal but they're soldiers, this is a war. We just aren't used to it yet."

I glare at Drummer. "We shouldn't have to get used to it. Are you prepared to kill someone, especially like that?" Drummer looks at his feet.

Luca looks apologetic. "They are the people who are going to get things done. If we want to make changes, we need to join with them." Jono and Drummer nod in agreement.

"And, for what it's worth, I don't think they'd ask anyone who wasn't prepared to, you know, go to those extremes to actually do that kind of stuff. It's not a gang where you need to prove yourself. As far as they're concerned we already have. Rescuing the leader of our nation, was a pretty lucky break on our part." Jono looks at me.

Is Jono right? I don't like seeing people murdered, or the idea of it for that matter, but we are at war. Innocent people are dying every day, the GDO slaughters thousands at a time. It doesn't mean killing people is right, but if the Resistance has to kill GDO soldiers to save themselves and others then I would have to accept it. But, I don't have to like it and I definitely won't be doing it myself.

We begin winding our way up a mountain path, keeping off ridges so our silhouettes don't stand out. I have no idea where we were heading. I'm hoping towards Vayo where I can find comfort from my parents, where I can feel like a teenager again, and let them do the worrying for a change. At one point, Dune drops back to join us.

"I don't think we should head to Vayo yet, not with scouts still out there." Reluctantly, I agree. I can't bring the army to my parents or the others. We walk along the narrow paths of the lower mountain until we come to a lush valley. The evening light draws long shadows across the landscape and, across the way, Drummer points out Vayo to me.

Vayo is a pretty town set against the backdrop of a luscious green valley with a river cutting it off from the abundant fields. The pitched grey roofs and white walls wink at us through the trees in the fading sunlight. An old ruin of an aqueduct runs into the town and up towards a ruined castle tower. Under any other circumstances it would be breathtakingly beautiful, even with the scars that pocket the buildings. I look across the valley with longing but turn towards the mountains and resume our gradual climb.

That evening we make camp in the yawning mouth of a cave. Luca is relieved to be off his leg, having walked the whole day without complaint. Someone lights a fire and Luca and I huddle together in the chill of the evening, listening to stories from past adventures of the Resistance. The stories they tell aren't about death and destruction, they are about hope, freedom, and camaraderie. They're fighting for the civilians, for their families, for those who can't fight back, for a just cause. I watch Dune and Echo as they laugh together, clearly devoted to each other, a unit.

Before we shuffle into our sleeping bags Dune turns to me. "You do understand the importance of what happened, don't you?"

"Meaning?" I ask.

"Meaning — you're the linchpin, Cassia."

I fall asleep with his words pressing in on me.

We spend the next few nights in the mountains, always moving throughout the day, constantly on the lookout. I learn the basics of hiding our tracks and get better at walking quietly. I begin to get to know Echo and Dune and I like them, even though I'm still sickened by what I have seen. We start to know the others as well; Ian was an accountant once, but now he's the unassuming assassin. No one suspects him because he looks so normal, so forgettable. He's the only one who makes me truly nervous because I will never know the things he's done and I know that there are many. Despite that, I feel comfortable with this group of rebels; it feels like an expansion of our small Sault team. It makes it seem like there is so much more that we can achieve if we work as one.

WEEK SEVENTEEN

We finally begin to make our way back to Vayo, to our families and the rest of the Resistance. Our food supplies are running low and so no matter how cautious we want to be, necessity brings us back.

The last few hours of our trek to the valley are the hardest for me. The weight of what has happened, the loss, the sorrow, and the weight of what's to come, make my feet leaden. When Vayo is in sight I feel dread, not relief. It's so quiet; what if the GDO has found them? It's dark as we approach. We can't hear a sound until someone steps from the shadows.

"Good to see you, Dune."

"You too, Ham." They slap each other's backs.

"Everyone's well, anxious for your return."

We walk along the cobbled streets until we come to a square filled with people. My parents and Luca's rush towards us — a sheepish-looking Ellyas steps forward, and Luca holds him in a brotherly embrace. Yve also approaches slowly, but more to give my parents room. She hugs me and then whispers in my ear, "Emma's here." I pull away and follow Yve's gaze.

In a shadowed doorway is the last of Jake's family. I approach her slowly, greeting people as I go. I don't say anything as I stand before her, just pull her to me, and she flings her arms around my neck and sobs painfully. I don't know how long we stand like that but eventually my mum approaches and coaxes Emma from me.

"I think Cassia is probably very tired, she's had a hard few days. Shall we show her to our place?"

"You've taken her in?"

"Of course." I hug my mother, infinitely grateful for her generosity.

I walk with my parents and Emma towards a small town house where another family occupies the bottom rooms, just like when we lived in Amphora. Up the stairs at the back of the house are two rooms: one for my parents, and one for Emma and me. My body is exhausted but my mind still races. My parents and Emma go to bed but I can't sleep; instead, I creep outside and make my way back to the square.

There, black against the inky rich sky, is Luca. I slip my arm around his waist and look up at the stars.

"Even though it wasn't for long, I still can't help but be grateful to be under the open sky." He sighs and I rest my head on his arm.

"Me too… Don't you find the more you look the more it feels like the universe is expanding before you? Like new stars keep appearing and there are layers and layers out there?"

He nods. "I keep thinking about what we should do, whether or not we really should join them."

"And?" I close my eyes, absorbing the moment.

"I want to keep fighting."

I let out a long, slow breath. "So do I." I have realised, later than I should have, that the freedom of my nation, of our people, is just as important as freedom for my family.

"At least this time you can't get upset because you 'think' you dragged me into it." He kisses the top of my head affectionately.

"Yeah, this time it's your fault."

"No, I think it was a mutual decision."

"So no one's to blame if we end up in prison again?"

"Nope."

I look back up at the ever-expanding universe. "You know, we could die".

"We could just as easily die hiding out here." True. I let the night's breeze cool my face as I stand with Luca wondering what is to come, trying not to think about what has been.

Eventually I go back to my room, but I lie awake for a long time, struggling to shut off my mind.

What keeps me up at night now isn't fear of the GDO, it's fear of who I am becoming. My great confession, the thing that I can barely admit to myself is this: I wanted to save Jake, I wanted to save all the innocent people in the building, but I also wanted all the GDO leaders dead. I wanted them gone and that's what frightens me, because before all of this, I would never have seen murder as justifiable. I believe in our justice system, in prison sentences — not in capital punishment. Before all this I would have baulked at murder but now, I'm glad they are gone, that they are dead. And that terrifies me more than anything and keeps me awake at night, along with the screams of the innocent lives that were stolen away because of me. I am capable of murder, I know that now. I wouldn't have joined the Resistance if I wasn't, and neither would Luca. I have come to recognise the darkest part of myself and I am terrified of it, terrified I'll succumb to it.

Once again we are at war and I have placed myself at the centre of it.

Some people are born to fight; I wasn't, yet here I am.

Acknowledgments

Thank you to my parents, not just for bringing me into this world, which was very good of them, but for not having simultaneous heart attacks when I told them I wanted to be an author. They've both supported me beyond measure. My brother James, thank you for fact checking and giving me horrifyingly disgusting insights into your time in the British Army. I'll never recover. My sisters, Sara and Rachel for being SISTERS that rock harder than Boyce Avenue, love you two enormously. My nieces and nephews for occasionally still thinking I'm cool. Kaavya, your marketing advice has helped me so much, you're the best. Michaela, thank you for always allowing me to steal your trademark phrases and stories and write them up as my own. Keep living more than I do so I continually have material.

Huge thanks to Cressida Downing for editing Rebellion, you gave me confidence in my work so that I could go ahead with publishing. Pam Firth, you are the queen of proofreading, I am so happy you know what split commas and split infinitives are because I clearly don't have a clue. You made this book readable. Thank you. Chris Dudley, you made my book beautiful and I know that people do actually judge books by their covers and I have so much confidence in what they'll think when they see Rebellion.

Thank you to you, the reader, because you reading my book has been a dream of mine for a very long time.

And lastly, Jules. Sometimes you're right, not always, but you are always in my heart, like an atrial myxoma.

Lightning Source UK Ltd.
Milton Keynes UK
UKOW02f1958260616

277043UK00002B/10/P